G000095131

The Auspicious Time

The Auspicious Time

ZHANG ZHILU

UNICORN

First published by Unicorn
an imprint of Unicorn Publishing Group, 2023
Charleston Suite, Meadow Business Centre
Lewes, BN8 5RW
www.unicornpublishing.org

10 9 8 7 6 5 4 3 2 1

ISBN 978-1-911397-44-1

Design by Susana Cardona

Printed and Bound by Short Run Press, Exeter

Prologue | 7

CHAPTER ONE ~ Kindergarten | 9

CHAPTER TWO ~ Begonia Blossoms | 20

CHAPTER THREE ~ The Third Eye | 28

CHAPTER FOUR ~ The 'Good-er' on the Windowsill | 33

CHAPTER FIVE ~ Colourful Clouds in the Sky | 38

CHAPTER SIX ~ Grow Your Own Vegetables and Eat by Yourself | 45

CHAPTER SEVEN ~ A Primary School Student | 53

CHAPTER EIGHT ~ Ms Guan | 57

CHAPTER NINE ~ Lao Dezi at the Opposite Door | 63

CHAPTER TEN ~ Xizhimen | 67

CHAPTER ELEVEN ~ New Friend | 73

CHAPTER TWELVE ~ Mr Lao and the Elder Ms Lao | 79

CHAPTER THIRTEEN ~ The Milky White Tree | 86

CHAPTER FOURTEEN ~ The Small Black Date Chen Yanping | 90

CHAPTER FIFTEEN ~ Growing Pains | 98

CHAPTER SIXTEEN ~ Less Than Nine Years Old | 102

CHAPTER SEVENTEEN ~ Hold Mother's Hand | 107

CHAPTER EIGHTEEN ~ Honour | 112

CHAPTER NINETEEN ~ **Uncle Zhao From the Little South House** | *120*

CHAPTER TWENTY ~ **A Special Day** | *125*

CHAPTER TWENTY-ONE ~ **A Crow Drinks Water** | *130*

CHAPTER TWENTY-TWO ~ **The Story of the Coping Saw** | *133*

CHAPTER TWENTY-THREE ~ **Brother's Pigeon** | *139*

CHAPTER TWENTY-FOUR ~ **Brother's Eagle** | *146*

CHAPTER TWENTY-FIVE ~ **Aunt Yu** | *151*

CHAPTER TWENTY-SIX ~ **Parachute** | *156*

CHAPTER TWENTY-SEVEN ~ **Red Star Drawing Pin Commune** | *166*

CHAPTER TWENTY-EIGHT ~ **Lying Flower** | *171*

CHAPTER TWENTY-NINE ~ **Picture Book Bookstore** | *175*

CHAPTER THIRTY ~ **Forgive me, Little Xinzi** | *183*

CHAPTER THIRTY-ONE ~ **Filming** | *190*

CHAPTER THIRTY-TWO ~ **The Unquenchable Flame** | *197*

CHAPTER THIRTY-THREE ~ **A Medal** | *202*

CHAPTER THIRTY-FOUR ~ **A Bottle of Soda** | *206*

CHAPTER THIRTY-FIVE ~ **Campfire Party** | *211*

CHAPTER THIRTY-SIX ~ **The Ice in Shichahai** | *216*

CHAPTER THIRTY-SEVEN ~ **Sister Went to a Provincial Area** | *222*

CHAPTER THIRTY-EIGHT ~ **Brother Became a Worker** | *224*

Epilogue | *227*

COMMENT BY LI DONGHUA ~ **Gift of the Past** | *233*

Prologue

One day, when I was packing my things, I came across a yellowish-white cloth bag at the back of the bookcase. When I opened it, I saw that it contained a pile of colourful pebbles. Although their colours had faded, I immediately remembered how they had looked decades ago.

There was a transparent glass bottle at home, as tall as a soda bottle and as thin as a canned fruit bottle. The mouth of the bottle was small, and the glass stopper was also very delicate. The stopper and the mouth of the bottle were both opaque. The bottle contained coloured pebbles. Red, green, brown and yellow. The stones, the size of the pad of a little finger, were soaked in water, crowded together and unable to move. The stones were in the water, and the water was between the stones, creating a striking image.

For as long as I could remember, this bottle sat on the coffee table by the window. One year, two years, ten years, twenty years... I had tried to pull out the stopper several times to pour the stones out, but I couldn't open it. My mother once told me, while shaking her head, 'I can't open it either. These stones have been placed in the bottle and arranged to create a scene. If the bottle was to be opened and the stones scattered, it would become nothing.'

One year, an accident happened at home; someone knocked the bottle over, and it smashed onto the tile floor. The water came out, and the stones were scattered all over the floor. I squatted down without thinking, trying to pick up the stones and put them back into the broken bottle. Mother picked them up and put them into a small white cloth bag...

Today, I put the stones into water again, and it was just like meeting an old friend; the stones immediately turned shiny in the water and seemed to give off an aura as if they were breathing and alive.

Although they were small, each one was different from the others. The patterns and meandering lines on their surfaces were beautiful, and they were so natural that they seemed to speak to me. Looking at those long-lost stones, I suddenly felt that every coloured stone in front of me was a frozen moment from my childhood. They were so old and yet so fresh, so great and yet so small, so peculiar and yet so ordinary.

So, I found a bottle similar to the original, picked up the pebbles one by one, and put them in: red, green, brown, yellow... And, as my mother had said, when the stones were placed in the bottle, they formed a scene.

CHAPTER ONE

Kindergarten

It was the winter of 1948, and Beijing (known at that time as Beiping) was freezing. Water drops turned into ice.

The snow had melted after landing on roofs, but before the water could reach the ground, it froze halfway. There were several strands of icicles hanging under the eaves of every house, the oily smoke from the chimney had turned the icicles yellowish brown, and the icicles had not melted for a month.

In the mornings, no one wanted to crawl out of bed. It wasn't that people didn't get enough sleep; it was really that the room was terribly cold. Whether or not the briquette stove was on, the windowpanes were always covered with ice flowers, and their patterns were beautiful and strange. Of course, they were different every day, but, in general, they all looked like rows of densely-leaved silvery trees. Sometimes, there was a white bear in the woods, and if you looked closely, the white bear became more apparent. Sometimes it was not a bear, but several identical flying birds...

If a corner of the quilt was occasionally lifted, precious heat could be seen flowing out in wisps. With every exhalation, a thick fog would appear above the bed.

After a while, there would come the sound of tinkering with the stove followed by the voices of his father and mother. At this time, Little Auspicious would listen very carefully; he knew that what he would hear next would always be one of two answers, but still, every morning, he looked forward to finding out which one it would be.

"Didn't seal it up yesterday; it was off." This meant that the fire had been extinguished.

"It's all right; the fire will be on soon." That meant the fire was still going.

Every time he heard the latter, Little Auspicious felt that the room had become warmer, and his heart was full of hope.

Sealing the fire before going to bed was a technical task. If the seal was closed too tightly when the bottom coal burned out, the new coal would not start burning, and the fire would be suffocated; if the seal was too loose, the new coal would burn out in the middle of the night, and it would be icy cold in the morning. Four-year-old Little Auspicious knew the stove was difficult to manage. If the stove had to be re-lit on a cold morning, the house would not only be cold but would immediately be filled with ash and smoke.

At that time, the Western New Year was called the Solar Calendar New Year, and only a few people celebrated it. On the other hand, Chinese New Year, known as the Spring Festival, was regarded as a genuine festival.

The Spring Festival of 1949 was approaching, but the city of Beiping was dead quiet, and no one was thinking about the New Year. Businesses and schools were closed and few people worked during the twelfth month of the Chinese year. Pedestrians on the street were sparse, and there were even fewer people pulling rickshaws. Only two or three soldiers in yellow and grey military uniforms patrolled the street. Children spoke in

hushed tones; they could see the dazed expressions on the faces of the adults. Everyone was waiting silently, not knowing what would happen the next day.

The Chinese People's Liberation Army (PLA) had surrounded Beiping. The city's defenders were the Nationalist Party's troops commanded by Fu Zuoyi. 'Encircling but not fighting' was the PLA's strategy. Outside Xizhimen (West Gate), the sound of cannons could be heard from time to time, coming from the direction of Xishan (West Hill).

A curfew was imposed in the city of Beiping. People were not allowed on the streets after dark. (If people were kept off the streets during the day, it would be known as 'martial law'.)

Little Auspicious, whose formal name was Auspicious, lived with his family in a house in Dacheng Alley, not far from Xizhimen.

One morning, Little Auspicious heard knocking on the courtyard door and the ring of the doorbell. His father dressed hurriedly then went outside to open the door. The yard was long, so it took him minutes to walk from the house to the courtyard door. All this time, the knocking at the door didn't stop, so his father knew that something serious must have happened!

The person at the door was Uncle Zheng, his father's good friend. Uncle Zheng was tall and had a loud voice, with a thick accent from his hometown in Shandong.

His father let Uncle Zheng into the house. Uncle Zheng stomped his feet and rubbed his hands to warm them, then said, 'Every house on Little South Street is being occupied by soldiers...'

'The People's Liberation Army has entered the city?' his father asked.

Uncle Zheng shook his head. 'Fu Zuoyi's troops have withdrawn into the city – no fighting. You are close to Little

South Street, and your yard is so big; I'm afraid the troops will also come here.'

His father took Uncle Zheng's hand and said emotionally, 'Good friend! Thank you for thinking about us.'

Mother put her hands together. 'Thank you, Mr Zheng. Thank you, Mr Zheng.'

'If the troops come, don't worry. Don't be afraid. They will only stay in places that have extra space to accommodate them. During the day, they have to report for duty. At most, they will only cook in the house or something!' Uncle Zheng assured.

Father nodded repeatedly.

Uncle Zheng also especially spoke to Little Auspicious. 'Don't be afraid.' Little Auspicious didn't know what to say, but his mother quickly gestured to him. 'Thank you, Uncle Zheng!' Uncle Zheng left. Little Auspicious would never forget the way he had smiled at him.

One day, when Little Auspicious was still only four years old, his mother sent him to kindergarten. It was located at the east entrance of East Guanyin Temple Alley, not far from home, and was attached to Beiping Normal School – a very good school.

His mother was a housewife, but she was knowledgeable enough that she would be able to keep her child from getting behind with his homework.

That first day was difficult for Little Auspicious; he was not only lonely but also a little scared. Several of his friends had not come to kindergarten that day. He sat in the corridor, looking out at the sky beyond the north room. The north room was like a big temple, with red walls, green tiles, and large glass windows. There was a large locust tree at the back of the house. Its leaves had fallen, and its bare branches stretched over the roof to the sky. The kindergarten seemed quiet and empty. Little Auspicious looked forward to his mother coming to pick him up early.

After he had been waiting for what seemed like a long time, his mother finally appeared and led Little Auspicious out the kindergarten gate. His mother wore a blue woollen coat with a pair of black-buckled cloth shoes, and he thought she looked very beautiful. He immediately felt a lot more at ease.

'Madam, do you want a ride?' A rickshaw man who was walking east stopped when he saw Little Auspicious and his mother. Little Auspicious knew that his mother would not hire a rickshaw since they were not far from home. She only paid for transport for long journeys such as the trip to Xidan, and even then, she would only pay for a tram.

His mother had little money, so even if Little Auspicious were tired, he would only ask his mother to rest for a while before leaving.

Mother waved her hand dismissively and took Little Auspicious to the west side of Xiaocheng Alley.

'Madam, give me a price.' The rickshaw man did not want to give up; he turned the front of the rickshaw around and got himself ready to take passengers.

Mother waved her hand again. 'Sorry, sir, our home is not far, and we will be home soon.'

Their house was on Dacheng Alley, which was connected to East Guanyin Temple Alley by the meandering Xiaocheng Alley. A lot of interesting people lived there, and many exciting things happened there, too. Little Auspicious's good friend Zhang Jing'en lived in Xiaocheng Alley. Zhang Jing'en's uncle was a great calligrapher, but it would be a long time before Little Auspicious knew that. Children didn't know the difference between celebrities and ordinary people, let alone what it meant to be a calligrapher. When Little Auspicious entered the house and saw him, he would greet him as 'Uncle Zhang'. Little Auspicious thought that the yard of Uncle Zhang's house was tiny. He would often see Uncle Zhang in the yard washing his feet, with a footed copper basin and a snow-white towel in front of him.

As Little Auspicious was thinking about this, a tall and chubby man carrying a briefcase suddenly appeared in Xiaocheng Alley. He looked wealthy. He was wearing a new blue lab coat, and he was walking hurriedly. His face was flushed, as if he had been running from something, but his outfit wouldn't let him move any faster. When he saw the rickshaw, it was as if he had seen his saviour. He raised his hand and shouted, 'Rickshaw! Rickshaw!'

Little Auspicious's mother instinctively gripped his hand. He looked towards Xiaocheng Alley. Before he could see anything clearly, the sound of swearing came from the alley.

'What are you running for? Who are you going to go to? You might have popped out of a crack in some rotten rock! Why keep the money? To buy a coffin?'

A middle-aged woman with a majestic and high-spirited demeanour appeared at the entrance to Xiaocheng Alley, accompanied by a girl of fifteen or sixteen.

Little Auspicious's heart tightened, and fear immediately surged within him. He heard from his elder brother, Big Auspicious, that there had recently appeared in the area a mother-and-daughter pair of beggars and that they were both fierce and aggressive. They wanted only money, not food. You would be very unlucky if they caught up with you. If you did not give in to them, they would keep scolding after you, cursing your ancestors. They were bold enough to say the curses that ordinary people dared not say aloud, and they would follow you for several alleys. Most people did not want to be bothered by them, so they would give them some money – to avoid further misfortune. When they received money, the beggars would then go and buy meaty Chinese buns, which were better than what Little Auspicious ate.

Auspicious looked at the two beggars in front of him. From their clothing, they did not look like beggars at all. Although their clothes were not new, there were no patches on them. Although their imprecations were vicious, they scolded people in a leisurely and cadenced manner. Such ungodly swearing! They spoke as if they were having an interesting conversation. This was unacceptable behaviour. Most people certainly did not want to provoke them.

Auspicious did not want to enter Xiaocheng Alley, so he pulled on his mother's hand and tried to head west. "Let's go this way."

His mother didn't speak, but Little Auspicious felt her hand grip his even more tightly. They did not turn but walked straight into the alley.

When the beggars saw them coming, their haranguing of the man stopped; without any surprise or uneasiness, they took a break from their scolding. Then, after about ten seconds, they resumed scolding him.

The distance to the beggars was small, but to Auspicious it seemed to take forever to reach them. He could not wait until they had passed them. He looked only at their feet, daring not to look any higher. When they came close, his mother took his other hand and moved him to her right side to keep Little Auspicious away from the beggars.

When they passed them by, Little Auspicious breathed out in relief. He couldn't help but turn his head to see what the 'danger' looked like now. However, he had not expected the girl to turn around as well.

The girl was not ugly. Compared to the women Little Auspicious had seen, this girl was rather good-looking. Strange, such a good-looking person; how could she be so vicious and aggressive? Suddenly, the girl shouted at Little Auspicious. 'What are you looking at? What are you looking for?'

Little Auspicious was stunned.

His mother stopped, turned sharply and scolded, 'Why are you scaring a child?'

The girl was startled. Little Auspicious's heart was in his throat, and he couldn't help but cling to his mother's leg.

Unexpectedly, the girl suddenly grinned. "What's wrong with me? I'm teasing him. Isn't it alright to tease?"

'Pretty lass, but what a pity...' said his mother, slowly enunciating each word.

The girl's mouth moved, but she didn't speak. Little Auspicious saw a trace of surprise and a little kindness in the eyes of the girl. Her mother was about to open her mouth, but before she could say anything, the girl turned and dragged her away.

Looking at the backs of the mother and daughter, Little Auspicious felt very strange. They didn't quarrel with his mother. Why did they leave without a word?

The melodious sounds of pigeon whistles could be heard overhead. Little Auspicious looked up and watched as a flock of pigeons – each bird with a traditional bamboo whistle tied to its tail – flew across the blue sky and swooped towards the steep eaves of Guanyin Temple. Then, as they flew up into the sky, the sounds of the whistles gradually faded away. (At that time, there were only a few tall buildings in Beiping. When one looked up, one could see the whole sky.)

For the next day or two, Father prepared for the troops to move in, including cleaning the vacant room in the backyard, but the troops did not come.

Later, everyone heard that General Fu Zuoyi and the People's Liberation Army had signed an agreement for the peaceful liberation of Beiping. On that day, according to the agreement, the Nationalist troops withdrew into the city of Beiping, and the People's Liberation Army troops took over the outside of the city. The Nationalist forces needed accommodation when they entered the city. They were temporarily accommodated on the street near the city wall in Xizhimen.

One day in February 1949, Beiping was peacefully liberated! The PLA entered at Xizhimen, and the people living in that area of the city felt very honoured. Beiping City returned to its former peaceful mood.

A few days later, a piece of news spread among the local neighbours: a rickshaw man who had been working near East Guanyin Temple was a prominent underground member of the Communist Party. Following the liberation of Beiping, his identity could be made public. He no longer needed to be a rickshaw driver and was now an official of high rank! It was thought that he might have become the mayor of the Xicheng District. These kinds of legends spread quickly amongst the children, many of them saying that this worker was from their alley. What did he look like? People said that he was simple and honest and had a white handkerchief around his neck, and there was nothing special about him except that he was nice to people.

Auspicious also wondered if he was the rickshaw worker who had greeted him and his mother that day.

On 1 October 1949, the People's Republic of China was established. That afternoon, Little Auspicious was listening to the radio from outside the door to Uncle Dong's house. There was a male announcer with a lovely voice, and Uncle Dong explained, 'This person is called Qi Yue...'

In September of that year, Beiping City was renamed Beijing City and became the capital of New China.

One day, Big Auspicious told his little brother that he had heard that the mother-and-daughter beggars had both gone to a cooperative on the same street to make matchboxes. Little Auspicious felt a burst of joy in his heart. He would no longer be afraid on the way to kindergarten.

CHAPTER TWO

Begonia Blossoms

Winter was over; spring had arrived. Many families were relieved that they no longer had to pay for coal for heating. However, a simple but silly question was often discussed in small talk: was winter better than summer?

There were many discussions; usually, people felt winter was better than summer, but in winter, people thought summer was better. Little Auspicious was most convinced of his mother's conclusion: 'Regarding living conditions, the rich have a good time in summer and winter, either way. But it is always difficult for the poor, who have a hard time in both summer and winter. The only difference is that summer does not freeze people to death.'

Little Auspicious remembered back to one of the hottest lunchtimes of summer, when the alley was deserted. The light shimmered faintly as the heat rose from the ground. The big locust tree at the west entrance of the alley looked lonely, and 'Futian'er' cicadas called out 'Futian'er! Futian'er!' desperately. The whole world seemed to be taking a nap.

Little Auspicious remembered how uncomfortable the summer evenings were, especially when the weather was 'holding back the rain'. The air was motionless, and even when people just sat still, sweat would trickle down their necks. The adults would sit in their yards with palm-leaf fans, fanning and fanning until midnight. And then, when a breeze began to blow, chilling their sweat, everyone would go inside.

Little Auspicious asked his mother, 'Are we rich or poor?'

His mother smiled wryly and said, 'Our family is an empty shelf. We are not rich, but compared to those who starve, we are not the poorest...'

The 'empty shelf' to which his mother referred was the yard of their house. It was a large yard, with a rockery in the middle to separate the front from the back. Based on the appearance of the yard, Little Auspicious's family would be considered rich, although the inconspicuous courtyard door did not give that impression. But as soon as the double wooden doors with peeling pale pink paint were opened, guests entering the courtyard for the first time were always surprised.

As the Chinese saying goes, 'Open the door and the mountain appears immediately', and that was an apt description of the scene that unfolded when one entered the courtyard. Most people said they were going out to see the mountain, but for those visiting Little Auspicious and his family, they came in to see a rockery.

One could vaguely see the houses and trees in the front yard through gaps between the rocks in the rockery. The whole rockery pattern was a cross: when you opened the door – horizontally it acted as a screen wall; vertically it divided the large yard into two. There were Western-style houses along the far edge boundary.

A roofed pathway connected the whole house. All of the windows were plastered with '米'-patterned sheets of paper to prevent shattered glass from flying far and hurting people during air raids.

On the right side of the rockery was a path paved with grey square bricks. To the right of the path was a lawn on which there grew a blanket of white peonies. A pink begonia tree leaned against the courtyard wall. When the peonies and the begonia were in full bloom, Little Auspicious thought he could hear the whispering voices of the flowers and plants nearby...

Unlike the traditional quadrangle courtyard houses that were common in Beijing, Little Auspicious's house and yard were Western in style. According to his father, Little Auspicious's father's elder brother had bought the house before the Anti-Japanese War. Unfortunately, before they could move into the house, the Japanese forces had instigated the Lugou Bridge Incident and occupied Beijing. In addition to the Japanese soldiers, many Japanese civilians also lived in Beijing. Four Japanese families lived in the courtyard house, and it was remodelled. In each family's living quarters was installed a toilet that could be flushed, and there was a large wooden bucket in the storage room next to each bathroom — Little Auspicious's father said that Japanese people bathed in such wooden buckets. The living room was huge, with sliding doors that opened out onto the front yard. When they were opened, you could see two upper and lower grids, made of tatamis.

The south room served as a communal living room for the four families.

When Little Auspicious's family moved in, the last Japanese family was still living there. They lived in the large living room next to the front yard. There was a girl in that family; her name was Mary. Mary's eyelashes were long, and her eyes were big and dark. Little Auspicious never saw Mary's mother; he only saw Mary's father occasionally smoking a pipe in the yard.

Mary's father was very polite to Little Auspicious, but he severely disciplined his daughter. Many times, Little Auspicious heard Mary crying in the yard when she was being punished. Sometimes, even the whistling of the belt could be heard. To this day, Little Auspicious still doesn't know why Mary was beaten.

Little Auspicious lived next door to Mary. Whenever he heard Mary's cry, the '米' pattern on the windowpane was particularly blinding. Little Auspicious tried to open the door several times to see Mary but was stopped by his mother.

When talking to his mother about these things, his mother always sighed and said, 'They have surrendered and are going back to Japan. They beat their children when they are upset.'

'Where's Mary's mother?'

His mother shook her head. Seeing that his mother didn't speak, Little Auspicious didn't ask anymore. He guessed that Mary's mother had probably passed away.

His mother would always talk about her brother – Little Aspicious's uncle. She told him that Little Auspicious's uncle had opened a restaurant called 'Taihe' in his hometown, Jinan, Shangdong, which was the county seat. One evening during the Japanese occupation, a Japanese customer got drunk and put a commando knife to his uncle's neck and threatened to kill him. His uncle was terrified, and he lay in bed with a high fever that night. Less than a month later, his uncle passed away. He was only in his thirties!

His mother said that in the countryside, the situation for villagers would be even worse than for those living in Jinan. Japanese soldiers would make a woman strip naked, then they would hang bells on her breasts and make her dance on a hot *aozi* (a tool for making pancakes).

Every time mother said this, she always exhaled and looked very angry.

The house in the front yard had a semi-basement, so the floor of the house was much higher than the ground, and one had to go up eight steps to enter it. When Little Auspicious was bored, he would often jump up the steps, hoping Mary would come out the living room door. They were the only two children living in the yard. Mary was a little older than him, maybe by two years.

When it rained, many snails would appear in the yard – bluish-grey in colour and the size of a fingernail. Children in Beijing called them 'niu' ('water buffaloes'). The poor 'buffaloes' were often used in cruel games. The children would each pick up a snail and try to crush each other's snail using the sharpest part of the shell. And, of course, the shell of the largest snail was the hardest.

When he was alone, Little Auspicious would spend most of his time watching a 'buffalo' emerging from its shell, first its 'horns', then its body, and then he would watch it as it climbed up the moss-covered wall, leaving behind a shining trail.

Little Auspicious often thought that the two horns of the 'buffalo' were the most magical things in the world. They were so soft and yet so straight when they stretched out. Where did they go when the 'buffalo' retreated into its shell?

Little Auspicious taught Mary to sing the song of the 'buffalo': 'The buffalo, the buffalo, the horns first come out and then the head, the roast mutton your parents bought for you... you don't eat it, it's for the cat…'

Mary seldom went out to play in the street. One day, when the gate of the courtyard was open, Little Auspicious saw a few children playing hopscotch outside the gate, so he asked Mary to go out with him to play. Mary followed Little Auspicious to the street. The kids playing hopscotch were older than them, so they just stood and watched. Not knowing how long they had watched, suddenly Mary's father appeared behind them. He didn't say a word but pulled Mary back by the shoulder as if he were picking up a kitten, and he took her back to the house.

Little Auspicious suddenly felt that something was wrong. He ran home quickly and said to his mother, 'Mary is going to be beaten!'

Mother asked, 'Why?' and then followed Little Auspicious to knock on Mary's door. It was the first time they had ever knocked on her door.

The door opened, and Mary's father stood at the door. Mary stood blankly beside a stool.

'What is the matter, Mrs Auspicious?' Mary's father asked.

Somehow, his mother had a newspaper and a jar of pigment powder in her hand. She said to Mary's father, 'I have a relative who asked me to make a pair of shoes for their child. Her feet are the same size as Mary's. So I want to use Mary's as a reference.' As she was speaking, his mother spread the newspaper on the floor.

Little Auspicious was stunned. Hadn't his mother come to rescue Mary?

Mary's father nodded and said, 'Of course.' Then Little Auspicious's mother turned around and waved, and Mary walked up to her. She took off Mary's shoes and made her step on the newspaper. She used painting powder to outline Mary's feet on the newspaper, and told Mary that she was very sensible and well behaved. But she said nothing about Mary being beaten.

Little Auspicious motioned at his mother several times, but she didn't seem to see it.

After the outlines had been painted, Little Auspicious followed his mother out of Mary's house, feeling very uneasy.

Back home, he asked her why she had said nothing.

She said, 'Mama has already said it; you just didn't hear it.'

Little Auspicious still didn't understand.

The next day, Little Auspicious asked Mary if she had been beaten the previous day. Mary shook her head with a smile like the begonias blooming in the yard.

One morning about two months later, there was a knock at their door. Little Auspicious's mother went to open the door and saw Mary's father standing there with a wicker box and Mary beside him carrying a small bag. Mary was wearing a black coat, and the white shirt underneath made her eyes seem brighter. Mary's father held up a key and said, 'Mrs Zhang, we are returning to our country. Please keep the key. Thank you for your care!'

Little Auspicious's father came out. He took the key and asked, 'Would you like to take some dry food with you for the journey?'

Mary's father waved his hand. 'No, we already have something to eat. Thank you.' After speaking, Mary's father turned and walked down the steps with Mary. When they got down to the second step, Little Auspicious's mother suddenly said, 'Wait a minute. I have something else to give you.'

She turned and went into the house. After a while, she came out with a new pair of tiny black shoes and handed them to Mary.

Mary looked up at her father. Mary's father opened his mouth, but no sound came out, and he blinked blankly.

His mother put the shoes into Mary's hand and said, 'Take them. You have a long journey ahead of you.'

Mary's father said, 'Sachiko, say thank you to Mrs Auspicious.'

Little Auspicious and his mother were both stunned for a moment. Wasn't she called Mary? Why did he call her Sachiko? They had never heard that name before.

Sachiko bowed to Little Auspicious's mother and held the shoes to her chest. Her father patted her on the shoulder, and the father-daughter pair turned away. Little Auspicious looked at their backs and felt a little uncomfortable.

"Sachiko is indeed a Japanese girl's name." said mother to herself.

Little Auspicious's father said quietly, 'Her real name is Sachiko. Maybe her father called her "Mary" because he feared people would hate her because she was Japanese.'

Little Auspicious suddenly ran out. He wanted to see what it was like to see Sachiko walking side by side in the alley with her father. He ran to the gate and saw a big truck. The truck had no hood, and some adults were already standing. He needed to find out where Sachiko was.

Little Auspicious shouted, 'Sachiko!'

The truck started. A small figure flashed out from behind several adults. Little Auspicious saw that it was Mary. Just like the day her shoe size was measured, a smile like a begonia blossomed on her little face.

CHAPTER THREE

The Third Eye

Little Auspicious could not remember eating many delicious things when he was a child. Life was tough during his childhood. His mother would often sing this ditty about his hometown:

We celebrate the Chinese New Year,
and we are not greedy for meat.
One day we will have a good time;
every day is the fifteenth of every month of the year.

One day, the neighbour from across the alley, Aunt Guo, came to borrow something from Little Auspicious's mother. What did she borrow? 'Big oil' – the oil 'refined' from fatty pork. Aunt Guo said that when her eldest daughter came back to visit, she wanted to make a dish which would be more fragrant if cooked with big oil. His mother took a small brown porcelain jar from the kitchen and handed it to Aunt Guo. Aunt Guo repeatedly said, 'No need, just give me two spoonfuls.' Finally, his mother took out a plate and dug out three spoonfuls of white oil from the jar, giving them to Aunt Guo.

The family would buy some suet or fatty meat every month and put it in the cooking pot to 'refine' it. After fat turned into a transparent liquid, it was poured into a small porcelain jar, where it would cool and solidify into a milky white lard. Little Auspicious's mother would tip the residue in the refining pot into a small dish, then sprinkle it with a little salt and pass it to him to eat.

Little Auspicious found it very fragrant and delicious.

It was almost noon when Aunt Guo came again. She brought a handful of small carrots with green leaves and handed them to his mother, 'Somebody gave me these. Wash and eat them; they're crunchy and sweet.' His mother said, 'Oh, Aunt Guo, why are you so polite? Three tablespoons of oil are not worth this much.'

Aunt Guo waved her hands repeatedly. 'Good neighbours don't talk about this.' Then she turned and walked away. Aunt Guo was a little chubby and had lotus feet (the result of foot binding in the old society), so walking quickly was quite challenging for her. Little Auspicious's mother always said in a grateful tone, 'I have to thank your grandma for not binding my feet. She disapproved of it. I have normal feet, and I even got to go to school.'

While eating radishes, Little Auspicious's elder sister told their mother, 'You should learn from Grandma.'

Their mother said, 'What's the matter? Did I bind your feet?'

His elder sister's voice became quieter. 'You prefer sons to daughters.'

'How do I prefer boys over girls?'

'You gave birth to Little Auspicious and made him light, while you made me dark.'

Their mother grinned, unsure if she should laugh or cry, and said, 'You are saying this at home. If you said it outside, wouldn't people think you are a fool? Is it my decision to make you black or white?'

'I'm just saying it. It's too late anyway.'

'You have a stubborn temperament. Can't you say something to please your mother?'

According to Little Auspicious's mother, his elder sister was good at everything, but she had a stubborn temper. No wonder her zodiac sign was the ox! When his elder sister made a mistake and was beaten with a feather duster or a broom, she never asked for mercy, and sometimes she didn't even cry.

'Despite my stubborn temper, I am still your child,' his elder sister muttered softly.

'Don't you think it would be easier if you asked for forgiveness?' Aunt Guo would often ask her. His sister nodded, but she would still be stubborn the next time. Their mother said a good temper brought good life, while a bad temper brought bad luck.

His sister was born in 1937, the year the Japanese devils instigated the Lugou Bridge Incident and the year the eight-year war of resistance began. Little Auspicious was eight years younger than his sister, and he was born in the days of the victory in the Anti-Japanese War.

All his sister's bad luck seemed to be because she was born in that painful, tragic year. Although they were born to the same mother, she had dark skin and Little Auspicious had white skin.

His elder sister often asked their mother, 'Why did you make my skin so black? What is the use of Little Auspicious being so white?'

Upon hearing this, their mother smiled helplessly and said, 'When I was pregnant with you, I ran all day, hiding everywhere and not eating, sleeping, or feeling well. This is a coincidence. Also, you are not too dark!'

Little Auspicious's sister was still angry. She pouted for a long time without speaking, with tears in her eyes.

At that time, there were no snacks at home other than dates and sunflower seeds grown in the yard. One year, their mother rubbed sunflower seeds off a flower tray, put them in a pocket-sized gauze satchel, and hung them in a hut next to the kitchen. During the festival, she brought it out so that they could fry and eat the seeds, but, unfortunately, only the shells of the seeds remained; the kernels were gone. Everyone knew that mice must have done this. Their mother said with emotion, 'People can't be so thorough.'

Little Auspicious's sister would often take out a few iron broad beans from the side pocket of Big Auspicious's clothes and give them to Little Auspicious. They were called 'iron' for a reason: when biting into one of them for the first time, it was the same as biting on a copper coin. Only by tenacious chewing and being soaking by the inexhaustible supply of saliva of a greedy child would the iron broad beans finally soften into a fragrant food.

Candy was rarely eaten at home. One day, Little Auspicious asked, 'Sister, do you have any fruit candy? I want some.'

His elder sister shook her head and looked around. The adults were not at home, and neither was Big Auspicious. His elder sister said, 'Wait, let me make candy for you.'

Little Auspicious then witnessed his sister's 'cooking skills'. While the adults were away, she lit the cooking sugar in a large copper spoon on the stove. After the sugar had melted, she poured it onto a pre-prepared glass sheet, and the sugar flowed naturally into the shape of a cloud. Before the sugar solidified entirely, she drew grids with the back of a kitchen knife on the 'cloud' so that it would be easier to eat later. The piece of candy was amber-coloured, and it was not only sweet in the mouth but also had a very fragrant caramel taste.

On that day, when his sister was heating up the sugar, Little Auspicious moved a square stool next to the stove to see her cooking skills. At that time, his sister was a primary school student, and Little Auspicious was not yet four years old. As he was watching, Little Auspicious suddenly fell and knocked his forehead on the corner of the stool, and blood began to flow from his forehead.

His sister was terrified and started crying. Although she was not beaten that night, she kept crying. She felt that she had hurt her brother. A month later, Little Auspicious's wound had healed, leaving a large scar on his forehead which resembled the god Erlang's third eye like a tiny grain of rice.

Little Auspicious learnt an old Beijing greeting in childhood: *Have you eaten?* This greeting worked on all occasions except, of course, when going to the toilet. In those days, eating a full meal was not only very important but also very difficult to do.

CHAPTER FOUR

The 'Good-er' on the Windowsill

The backyard of Little Auspicious's house was huge, and the north house was rented out to a Mr Nan ('Nan' means 'south'). He was the director of a radio training school. Less than a month later, Mr Sun's family moved into the west house in the backyard. At that time, Little Auspicious seldom went to the backyard. Mr Sun's family had a daughter who attended Sicun Middle School. Several times, Little Auspicious tried to talk to her, but before he could get close, she just left as if he didn't exist at all.

The house from the front yard to the backyard bent around the rockery. Through the west-facing windows of the front yard, one could also see the backyard.

There were more houses in the front yard than in the backyard, and the backyard was bigger than the front yard.

One day, the yard suddenly became lively, and many policemen in yellow clothes came. They all went to the backyard. Little Auspicious stood at the corner of the corridor to watch what was happening, and his mother held his hand tightly.

The door of Mr Nan's house was open, but there was no one inside. The door of Mr Sun's house was also open, but Mr Sun was nowhere to be seen. The policemen were moving things out of the room. After a while, Little Auspicious saw Mrs Sun coming out holding a bundle and followed closely by her daughter. Mrs Sun was crying. Mrs Sun's daughter held tightly onto her mother's woollen vest. Little Auspicious watched intently as they walked across the yard, passed through a passage in the rockery, and then walked out through the gate.

When passing through the rockery, Mrs Sun glanced at Little Auspicious and his mother. She dared not speak, and his mother dared not ask, but something terrible must have happened to their family.

Two days later, in the afternoon, Big Auspicious came back home, and when he came through the door, he said to his father, breathlessly, 'Dad…I saw Mr Nan... I saw him in Houhai... He was tied to a truck in Houhai….'

It took a while for his brother to explain that Mr Nan was a military agent of the Nationalist Party. He had been tied to a truck, paraded in the streets, and then shot. Later, news came that Mr Sun was also a spy. He did not belong to the National Bureau of Investigation and Statistics (Military Commission) like Mr Nan; he worked for the Central Bureau of Investigation and Statistics. A two-way radio had been found in his house. Little Auspicious never heard anything more about Mr Sun, let alone where his wife and daughter had gone.

Both Mr Nan's and Mr Sun's homes were sealed. There was no sound in the backyard. It was so quiet that it scared people, even in broad daylight.

'Two spies from the same backyard, one in the Central Bureau and one in the Military.' One day, Little Auspicious's mother whispered to his father, 'Is this true? Is it because of bad feng shui?'

His father said nothing, pointing to Little Auspicious and his sister, as if to imply she should not talk about these things in front of the children.

A month later, the seals were lifted. Everything in the houses was removed.

No one lived in the backyard, and as it was not rented out again, the yard remained deserted.

A few days later, Little Auspicious's father put several chickens on the slope next to the south house in the backyard. From then on, the first sound Little Auspicious heard every morning was the sound of a rooster crowing, and the backyard finally came to life again.

When heard the hen clucking, Little Auspicious knew it had just laid an egg, so he would run to the chicken coop. If the hen was still sitting on the nest, Little Auspicious would shoo it away, leaving behind a still-warm egg. It was a happy and delightful discovery.

One particular incident left a deep impression on Little Auspicious. One day, when he came in through the gate and walked to the backyard, he saw what looked like an old raven flying past the mulberry tree with a piece of yellow cornbread in its mouth. Then he took another look and thought that perhaps it was carrying a nest. In fact, it was an eagle that had taken away a little fluffy chick from the henhouse! From then on, whenever the chickens were allowed out of the henhouse, there had to be someone watching them. Later, barbed wire was strung over the top of the chicken coop.

Maintaining such a large yard made life at home more and more complex. Little Auspicious's family moved to the backyard, intending to rent out the front yard. The Lao family moved in in the summer of the following year. This change was a major upheaval for Little Auspicious and his family.

Every time he went out, Little Auspicious's father would go in his own rickshaw. The master who pulled the rickshaw, Old Li, was about forty years old. No one called him 'Uncle Li'; everyone in the family called him 'Old Li'. In Little Auspicious's mind, after his parents and elder brother and sister, Old Li was the closest person in his family.

Old Li called Little Auspicious's father 'Master Five' and his mother 'Madam'. Old Li had originally been a mason. His father first met him in 1945, after victory had been won in the Anti-Japanese War. His father saw that he was a nice person, so he asked him to pull a rickshaw for him rather than work as a mason. Old Li decided to serve Little Auspicious's father. In addition to pulling rickshaws and doing household chores, as long as he was needed for something, he would never refuse. Old Li became the family's housekeeper. Old Li pulled rickshaws for Little Auspicious's father from the year the Anti-Japanese War was won until 1951, the year Mr Lao moved in.

The life of Old Li's family was tough. Old Li's wife suffered from an eye disease, possibly cataracts, that made her half-blind. She had a bad temper, but this had not prevented her from having five children.

One day, Little Auspicious's father gave Old Li twenty yuan and said to him, 'I will not be using the rickshaw anymore, and I am terribly sorry, old chap, that I can't continue to employ you. You could take the rickshaw with you – please feel free to be a freelance rickshaw driver or do masonry again.'

Tears began to well up in Old Li's eyes. He put the money on the table and said, 'Master Five, please do not feel so sorry. The years I've been working with you have been the happiest years of my life. When you have money, I'm here, and if you don't, I leave. If that is the case, what kind of person am I?'

Little Auspicious's father smiled wryly, 'Old Li, I won't let you go if there is a way, but as you can see, the family will starve. Can I still afford to take the rickshaw?'

Old Li insisted that he did not want their money. He sold the rickshaw and gave the money to them. Little Auspicious's father insisted that Old Li take the money with him. Old Li was overcome with emotion at the generosity shown him. He stayed at the house for several more days before resuming work as a mason.

One late evening during the Mid-Autumn Festival that year, Old Li came unannounced to Little Auspicious's house, but the whole family had already gone to bed. Old Li said, 'Master Five, today is the Mooncake Festival. I had planned to come earlier, but I had a job I couldn't refuse. Now that I have finished work, I have come to visit.'

Little Auspicious's father said, 'Everybody is asleep. Let's chat tomorrow.'

'Well then, Master Five, have a good rest. I will put this "good-er" on the windowsill for you.'

The sound of voices had woken Little Auspicious. He heard rustling and the sound of footsteps as Old Li walked away. Then he heard the distant sound of the courtyard door closing.

I will put this 'good-er' on the windowsill for you. Little Auspicious thought this sentence was amusing and couldn't help but feel moved.

The next morning, Little Auspicious went to the windowsill to have a look, but there was nothing there. He said to his father, 'There is nothing!' His father smiled and said, 'How come you say there is nothing?'

'What is there?'

'There is a "good-er"!'

CHAPTER FIVE

Colourful Clouds in the Sky

In Beijing, there were very few large yards that did not have jujube trees. There was a jujube tree in front of the house where Little Auspicious lived. One of its horizontal branches ran parallel to the eaves. From the jujube tree blooming to the flowers changing into small green fruits and then the tiny green fruits turning into red and green jujubes hanging on the branches, everything was vivid in Little Auspicious's mind.

In autumn, when his father said, 'It's time to make jujubes!' it was a mobilisation order. His elder brother climbed the tree, and everything from the big washbasin to the small rice bowl came in handy, because all the neighbours would be given one portion. Little Auspicious felt the happiest during the jujube harvest. He brought jujubes in a small basin to each of the neighbours. They would say, 'Thank you', and he would say, 'You are welcome!' It was so simple, yet so enjoyable!

In the backyard, there were two grapevines about five metres apart, one to the north and the other to the south. In winter, Little Auspicious's father cut the main branches of the vines, coiled them up and buried them in the soil, forming a pile. In spring, the branches were dug out, and the soil was piled up to become a 'water basin' for the vines. His father built a wooden trellis between the two grapevines. Little Auspicious's job was to water the vines every day. At first, the branches barely reached the trellis, but after about a week, new shoots started to grow up the trellis. Then the vines needed even more water. Little Auspicious watered them with buckets of water every afternoon after school. Day by day, he saw that the new branches and tendrils were covering more and more of the trellis. Then the leaves started growing out one by one, and small green buds began to appear—small grapes! The vines required the most water at this stage of their growth, and Little Auspicious's job became even more arduous. He poured the water every day, almost overflowing the 'basin' each time. It was hard work, but Little Auspicious was very happy. In the hot summer, it was very pleasant to move a bamboo chair and lie under the grape trellis and watch the branches cover each other and the leaves communicate with one another above his head. At noon, he would read a book under the grape trellis. Sometimes, he would fall asleep happily.

Unlike the wooden floor of the house in the front yard, the floor of the house in the backyard was paved with tiles. When she walked on the tiles for the first time, Little Auspicious's mother smiled and said, 'How wonderful! There is no sound when walking. How quiet it is!'

Shortly after they had moved to the backyard, Little Auspicious turned one year older. The world in front of him gradually became clearer, and it no longer seemed like a dream.

There was an old man who picked up rags in the alleys in the area. He would sometimes knock on the courtyard door, hoping to get some rags. Little Auspicious's mother often gave him steamed buns and pancakes. Every time, he always thanked her politely and decently, and he even praised Little

Auspicious several times when he saw him. He would often cut wastepaper into palm-sized squares on which to write calligraphy. One day, he brought a stack of these squares with writing on them and gave them to Little Auspicious's mother. The old man's origin was unknown, but the quality of his calligraphy was decent. Even Little Auspicious's father said it was very good. His mother put the papers in an old tin makeup box and used them to teach Little Auspicious how to read. It was his first set of literacy cards.

Gradually, he began to recognise the characters on the cards. His father was very happy with him and gave him a student dictionary. Little Auspicious, still only a kindergartener, quickly learned how to use a dictionary.

In addition, Little Auspicious also learned to sing the Ping operas that were popular at that time, such as *Liu Qiaoer* and *Little Son-in-law*, and the neighbours enjoyed it when he sang the songs to them.

At that time, 'Resist US Aggression and Aid Korea' became a major initiative in China. The People's Government said that the American Imperialists had invaded Korea and that China would aid the Korean people. Adults and children alike recited the slogan, 'Resist US Aggression, Aid Korea, Defend the Homeland and the Country.' Two songs were sung in government schools, streets and alleys. One song went like this:

> Hey la la la la, hey la la la la, the sky is full of colourful clouds! Red flowers are blooming on the ground! The people of China and North Korea are powerful; they defeated the American soldiers!

Everyone was more familiar with the other song:

> Be valiant and high-spirited, cross the Yalu River, and keep the peace for the motherland to protect your hometown, the good sons and daughters of China; move forward with one heart, unite as one, and defeat the wild wolf of the American Imperialists... Be valiant and high-spirited...

There was also a nursery rhyme not taught by the teachers that Little Auspicious and the other children all knew:

> One, two, three, four, five; go up the mountain to fight tigers;
> Tigers don't eat humans; they only eat Truman.

The children didn't know that Truman was the president of the United States at the time; they only knew that he was a big villain.

The kindergarten teacher helped the children to rehearse a small opera called *Aunt Zhu Delivers Eggs*. That day, the principal of the kindergarten came to personally select the actors for the show. There were three main roles: Aunt Zhu, a volunteer army soldier, and Truman. The story went as follows. Aunt Zhu fills a basket of eggs at home, then sings while walking on her way to giving the eggs to the volunteer army soldier. Truman appears, looking around and shaking his head. The soldier reappears, and behind him are Aunt Zhu and other villagers. Everyone steps forward together, and Truman runs away in a panic, falling to the ground in fright.

The lyrics of *Aunt Zhu* were as follows:

> The hen lays eggs! Cock-clack-cluck-cluck. Aunt Zhu collects the eggs and puts them in the earthen kiln. She walks two miles through Big Phoenix Village and comes to Big Stone Bridge... Give the eggs to relatives and volunteers, and then ask comrades to fight the war with good hard work...

The principal asked the children in the senior class to stand in two rows, and each child sang a song. After the singing, the principal asked, 'Who wants to be the volunteer soldier?' All the children raised their hands except for Little Auspicious. He was too timid. The principal said, 'Little Auspicious, can you raise your hand higher?' Little Auspicious had no choice but to raise his hand. In the end, the principal chose the tallest child in the class to play the volunteer army soldier. The principal then asked who would be willing to play Truman, and everyone looked at each other. Only Liu Guangting raised his hand to volunteer. The other children laughed. The principal smiled and asked, 'Why do you want to be Truman?'

'It's fun,' Liu Guangting replied.

The process of choosing Aunt Zhu was somewhat surreal for Little Auspicious. The ones who raised their hands were all girls, of course. Song Xiaohui raised her hand calmly, neither too high nor too low. The children all knew that the principal would choose Song Xiaohui because she was good at singing and dancing and was also good-looking. Little Auspicious never expected the principal to say, Let's ask Little Auspicious to play Aunt Zhu!'

Little Auspicious was taken aback. He had been selected to be Aunt Zhu. What had just happened? Liu Guangting shouted, 'Wow, a man to dress up as a woman!' There was nothing wrong with this sentence, but Little Auspicious felt it was mocking. Although he was timid, he didn't like others to describe him that way or to say that he was quick to cry. He was most afraid of others saying that he looked like a girl. But the principal had chosen him to play Aunt Zhu. Could it be that he really looked like a girl? He wanted to cry.

When school was over, the teacher told Little Auspicious's mother that he had been chosen to play Aunt Zhu.

The teacher's expression showed that this was something he should be happy about.

On the way home, his mother said, 'You should be happy.'

'I don't want to play a girl,' murmured Little Auspicious.

'Didn't Mei Lanfang only play female roles? How well he performed...'

Little Auspicious didn't speak. He felt awkward. Back home, his mother told the whole family about Little Auspicious's role as Aunt Zhu. His sister said, 'I knew it! Little Auspicious will definitely be romantic in the future. He can learn to sing!' Little Auspicious felt that the word 'romantic' was similar to 'rogue', so he snapped back, '*You* are the one who is romantic!'

His father patted him on the shoulder and said, 'Little Auspicious, this is a good thing! You have to practice everything so that you can gain insight!'

'I don't want to play a girl,' Little Auspicious whispered.

'There is nothing wrong with a man dressing up as a woman. Look at the four famous actors, Mei Lanfang, Shang Xiaoyun, Xun Huisheng, and Cheng Yanqiu. They are all men, but they play the female role brilliantly!'

'I don't want to learn to sing opera,' Little Auspicious said warily.

His father added, 'Is you not wanting to play the role of Aunt Zhu due to you being timid?'

Little Auspicious didn't speak.

His father laughed. His elder brother came over and said, 'Aunt Zhu delivering eggs is a folk song; it's easy to sing!'

Little Auspicious immediately asked, 'If they asked you to perform, would you do it?'

His brother nodded. His nod encouraged Little Auspicious greatly. He felt relieved, and he decided to play Aunt Zhu, dressed up like a woman.

In the next few days, Song Xiaohui lent him a flowered blouse, and his sister lent him a red turban. His older brother taught him how to cross step, and he sang as he walked.

On the day of the performance, his mother and many parents came.

The performance took place in the yard of the kindergarten. Little Auspicious wore a red turban. He had an apron around his waist and carried a small basket on his arm. He was Aunt Zhu. In addition to singing the lyrics, he said a few words then gave the egg to the most lovable person – the volunteer army soldier who resisted US aggression and aided Korea.

In addition to Little Auspicious's Aunt Zhu, Liu Guangting's Truman was brilliant, too. As soon as he came on stage, everyone laughed. Truman wore a top hat with the American flag pattern on it. When he introduced himself while walking crookedly, the yard was filled with laughter. In the last scene of the performance, Truman was so frightened by the roar of the crowd that he fell to the ground.

Little Auspicious's mother quietly asked the principal, who was sitting on the side, why Little Auspicious had been chosen to play Aunt Zhu. The principal looked at Little Auspicious with a mysterious smile and said, 'Isn't this very good?'

His mother had never looked so happy. For a long time, she said to everyone, 'You haven't seen Aunt Zhu played by our Little Auspicious. It was brilliant!'

CHAPTER SIX

Grow Your Own Vegetables and Eat by Yourself

Six-year-old Little Auspicious followed his mother out through the kindergarten gate for the last time. In his hand, he held a diploma rolled into a scroll with a purple ribbon tied around it.

The threshold for the gate was high. Every time Little Auspicious had walked through the gate, he had had to raise his knees high to step over it. This would be the last time he would have to cross the threshold.

'You are going to primary school; in this case, you shouldn't cry as much,' said his mother.

Little Auspicious nodded. Of course, he had grown up now.

His mother made him sit on a stone bench at the gate of a house. The stone bench was very strange; it was a pair of large white stone cubes with a quarter carved out to form a seat. Two such seats were placed at the gate, looking very majestic. Later, Little Auspicious heard from his mother that these seats were called Horse Mount Stone. A couplet on the gate read 'Loyalty is handed down to the family for a long time, and poetry and books will last forever.' Apparently, a great painter had once lived at that house.

Little Auspicious's mother took the graduation certificate from him, untied the ribbon, unrolled it, and asked him to read it out to her.

Diploma
Kindergarten Student Auspicious is from Zhucheng, Shandong Province, and he is six years old now. In this month of this year, the nursery period in this kindergarten expires, the examination results are passed, and the child is allowed to graduate.
This certifies.

Below was the principal's blue signature stamp.

At the top of the graduation certificate was an oval-shaped portrait of Chairman Mao, with yellow ears of wheat, two national flags and four flying white pigeons on both sides, and the silhouettes of a dozen children playing games below.

His mother said solemnly, 'You can recognise so many characters. If you hadn't cried so much, then you could have taken first place.'

When they got home, the house was empty. Little Auspicious's father was out, and his brother and sister hadn't finished school yet.

Little Auspicious moved a stool and sat under the jujube tree, looking at the sky. It was very blue and clear except for the occasional white cloud. He could hear pigeon whistles coming from far and near. He had heard from adults that there was no limit to the sky. Little Auspicious looked at the sky and felt very uncomfortable – how could something be endless? No matter how big something is, no matter how far away, there must be a boundary. How could the sky have no ends? Little Auspicious couldn't imagine what a thing without ends would look like.

But what if the sky had an edge? Then what was outside the edge? Thinking of this, Little Auspicious felt even more uncomfortable; he felt as if he were fighting with himself, stuck in a mud pit and unable to get out. It made him feel suffocated.

The doorbell rang outside, followed by the sound of the door opening. Little Auspicious knew that this was his father returning home. His father rang the doorbell not to ask for someone to open the door for him but to inform the family that he was back. Little Auspicious could hear his father beating his clothes with a duster in the hallway, as had been his habit for many years. Every time he entered the house, he would take the duster that hung on a nail in the corridor and use it to beat his clothes. He was the only one in the family who did this.

Little Auspicious hurried to the corridor. 'Dad, I graduated from kindergarten.'

His father smiled and briefly stroked Little Auspicious's face – this was how he expressed his love to him. When others touched Little Auspicious's face, they would hold his face in their hands, but his father was not like this. He would just touch his face briefly, and if Little Auspicious liked it, he would do it again.

But his father's face had a dark expression that day, and Little Auspicious could see that he was forcing a smile. When his mother told him that Little Auspicious had won third place, he touched Little Auspicious's face again, but he seemed distracted. His father was not usually like this.

At dinner, Little Auspicious's father said, almost casually, 'The house has been confiscated.'

Little Auspicious's mother froze for a moment, then put down her bowl and chopsticks and paused again before asking, 'Then what should we do?'

His father said, 'I have to go to Shanghai.'

Little Auspicious didn't understand what had happened, but he realised from his parents' expressions that it was serious. Little Auspicious's uncle owned the house. He had gone to Taiwan in 1949, and his family had stayed in Shanghai. Some people speculated that the house had been the property of the Japanese and that it should be confiscated and returned to the public.

After lunch, Little Auspicious said that he wanted to play in the street. His mother changed his shoes for him. Little Auspicious saw that the double-buckled shoes she put on his feet were his sister's old shoes. That they were old wasn't the problem; what he didn't like was that they were girls' shoes.

'These are girls' shoes! I don't want to wear them!'

'It doesn't matter. You aren't going to school. Besides, children's shoes are not divided into boys' and girls'. People won't laugh.'

'They look ugly!' Little Auspicious wanted to cry.

'You used to wear them, too. What's the matter today?'

'I've never worn girls' shoes!'

His mother said angrily, 'Why are you so ignorant? The family is almost out of food.'

It worked. Little Auspicious stopped arguing and ran out of the house wearing the girls' shoes.

During dinner, Uncle Zheng paid them a visit. In Little Auspicious's eyes, Uncle Zheng looked like a great Buddha. Not only was he tall and big, but he also always turned up when Little Auspicious's family was in trouble.

Uncle Zheng ate and drank wine. He spoke the Shandong dialect with a strong accent. Little Auspicious felt that dust was shaken down from the roof from time to time. His father also drank some wine, and his face turned as red as that of the great god Guan Yu. He said many things that Little Auspicious couldn't understand, only the colloquial words, 'Alas, if

I had a way…'Just that one sentence was deeply engraved into Little Auspicious's heart.

Uncle Zheng left. Little Auspicious's father pointed to a big white bundle on the bed and said to his mother, 'Uncle Zheng purposely left that mink coat behind.' Little Auspicious's mother just nodded, and it took a long time before she said, 'Uncle Zheng is really a good man!' Little Auspicious didn't know what a mink coat looked like, only that it was very valuable. From his parents' tone, he knew that it was a life-saving treasure.

Little Auspicious's father sold the mink coat left by Uncle Zheng, bought a plane ticket, and flew to Shanghai.

After a long time away, his father returned from Shanghai. The tense and silent atmosphere in the house gradually changed. Finally, one day, his father announced to the family that the house had been returned. On that day, although the meals were not much different from the past, Little Auspicious felt that the food was more delicious than usual. Everybody was very happy. His father also drank a glass of wine, and his face glowed red.

This was the time when Little Auspicious and his father spent the most time together. One day, his father changed into a double-collared white coat and a pair of black trousers pinched at the bottom like those of a martial artist. He carried several bundled sacks and led Little Auspicious out. They didn't get in the car; they just kept walking. They came to a grocery stall in Xinjiekou. His father sold the sacks and led Little Auspicious to another shop.

As he was walking in, Little Auspicious thought he was entering a grain store, but, unlike in a typical grain store, there were no piles of grain bags. Almost all the grain was placed in small cloth pockets lying opened on the ground.

Although the pockets were small, there were many varieties of grain: red, green, black, and yellow. Many of the grains Little Auspicious didn't recognise. Some grains were placed on a large plate on the counter, and the grains in the small individual glass boxes were colourful. Some were round like millet grains; some were like small water chestnuts; and some were small, black and ugly. Some had many edges and had small hairs on them.

'That's not food. These are carrot seeds.' Little Auspicious's father pointed to the seeds with small hairs.

On that day, Little Auspicious learned a lot. His father bought leek seeds, tomato seeds, eggplant seeds, and those interesting carrot seeds. The seed merchants sorted the seeds into small packets made from newspaper, with four sides and four corners, like paper *zongzi* (a type of dim sum).

When he got home, Little Auspicious was exhausted. He had never walked so much in such a short time. When he was in bed that night, his father patted his quilt and said, 'Little Auspicious, get up early tomorrow. I will teach you how to grow vegetables.'

Little Auspicious looked at his father curiously. How could he grow vegetables?

The next morning, his father led Little Auspicious to plough a field between the jujube trees and the grape trellises. His father dug the soil with a shovel in front, and Little Auspicious followed behind with a small coal shovel to break up the big pieces of dirt. A ridge of soil was piled up through the middle and around the whole field, dividing it into four small fields. Little Auspicious and his father worked for a whole day. In the evening, his father sowed the seeds that he'd bought the day before. He planted tomatoes, eggplants, leeks and carrots in the four small plots.

Since that day, Little Auspicious watered the vegetable field frequently and watched the seeds they had planted sprout, bloom and bear fruit. That summer, Little Auspicious's family ate predominantly the vegetables they had grown in the yard.

CHAPTER SEVEN

A Primary School Student

Little Auspicious was admitted to the Number Two Primary School attached to Beijing Normal University (Beishi Erxiao) and entered first grade.

Beishi Erxiao was a public school, and it was the best in the area. It held entrance examinations, and admissions were based on merit. Therefore, attending the school was something to be proud of. Little Auspicious's kindergarten buddies Liu Guangting and Song Xiaohui also entered the school and became his classmates again.

To the left of the path that led into the school, there was a white wall on which there was a map of the People's Republic of China. At the top of the map were the words 'China is one of the largest countries in the world!' There was a tall mirror next to the map, so that teachers and students could check whether their clothes were neat before they entered the school. Opposite the map was the window to the reception.

Primary school students in the first grade often didn't know where to go, so Little Auspicious went to the window, stood on his tiptoes and asked, 'Excuse me, steward. How can I get to the office?'

The man inside opened the small window and asked sternly, 'What did you say?'

Little Auspicious panicked a little. 'May I ask you something?'

'I know you're asking something. What did you call me just now?'

'Steward,' Little Auspicious murmured.

The man didn't seem happy. 'Who taught you that?'

Little Auspicious was stunned. He remembered that when going places with his mother, she would always address the doormen in that manner. Now he realised that there was something wrong with the title. But he didn't want to blame his mother, so he blushed and didn't speak.

The man looked stern and said, 'It's a new society now, you know?'

Little Auspicious nodded.

'"Steward" is what the wealthy called their servants in the old society, and they looked down on the working people. Now it is inappropriate. Why do you still call me "steward"? How did your parents teach you?'

Little Auspicious knew he was in the wrong. It would have meant nothing to him if he were a 'wild child'. But he was a very polite child. He could only say, 'I really don't know.'

The man said, 'You can call me "Teacher" or "Uncle" in the future. Understand?'

Little Auspicious nodded again.

The window slammed shut.

When he was in kindergarten, he had heard the teachers and parents call the gatekeeper 'Steward'. It seemed that primary school and kindergarten were different. When he had grown up, he realised that it was not that kindergarten was different from primary school but that the eras were different.

In those first few days, Little Auspicious was a little unlucky. In addition to being reprimanded by the uncle in the reception, he was also criticised outside the school.

Peiji Primary School was based in Xiaocheng Alley. On his way home from school, Little Auspicious always passed Peiji Primary School. There were high steps at the entrance to the school. It had no playground, just a pair of yards. It was not much bigger than a kindergarten. It was a private primary school at a time when people viewed public schools as better.

Whenever children passed by Peiji Primary School or met students from the school, they would shout, 'Peiji Primary School, everyone knows that the teachers are sweet potatoes and the students are yams!' Little Auspicious joined in, too.

One day, when they were walking past Peiji Primary School, Little Auspicious and a few classmates shouted their familiar insult. As they did, a middle-aged man came out of the school. He was wearing a blue gown and a felt hat that could be pulled down to cover his face. There was a button on the top of the hat. The classmates with Little Auspicious all ran away. The man stopped Little Auspicious and said, 'Student, why are you saying that? Did your parents teach you that?

Little Auspicious was always dumbfounded when he questioned by a stranger. He felt very scared and didn't know what to say. Besides, it was unkind to say that the teachers were sweet potatoes and the students were yams. He just stood there blankly.

The man asked again, 'Which school are you from?'

Little Auspicious said that he was from Beishi Erxiao. The man said, in a serious voice, 'I could go to your teacher, but I won't do it this time. But you must remember that no matter which school you go to, you must be a good student. Students must first be kind. No matter which school, everyone is equal. The teachers and students of Peiji Primary School did not bother you, nor did they provoke you. Why do you insult others? Isn't this bullying? Kind people never bully.'

The man's serious and somewhat sad eyes made Little Auspicious stop and think. He felt sorry for him, and he realised that he had done something wrong. Little Auspicious couldn't remember what happened next. Afterwards, he heard from his classmates that it was the principal of Peiji Primary School who had told him off. This incident left a deep impression on Little Auspicious.

CHAPTER EIGHT

Ms Guan

The house on the south side of the yard that one could see when entering through the school gate was the headquarters of the Young Pioneers. In front was a small courtyard. Looking ahead, there was a moon gate on the right. Past it were the principal's office, teachers' offices and dormitories. There were many lilac trees in front of and behind the house. The surroundings were beautiful and quiet.

There was also a moon gate at the front of the small courtyard. The teacher's kitchen and boiler room were on the left, and a water pump was on the right. If students felt hot or thirsty, they could press the water press twice, and cool water would flow out, sparkling in the sunshine.

The most exciting thing for the students was the big apricot tree in front of the water pump. The tree was enormous, and the apricots were also surprisingly large, as big as a first-grade student's fist. Whenever the tree bore fruit, people walking near the tree could smell an aroma that was both sweet and sour.

Through the front moon gate under the big apricot tree was the school's big playground. On the of the playground left was a two-storey grey brick building containing twelve classrooms, and on the right was a long single-level building housing six classrooms.

The school had strict regulations. There were two classes in each grade. Even though there were thirty-five students in each class, the classrooms were oversized. There were seats at the back for trainee teachers. Little Auspicious would often see many young teachers sitting in the back listening to the lesson, but if they weren't there, the classroom would appear empty, with a large open space at the back.

In the first week of school, seventy students from two classes came together to watch a Soviet film, *Primary School Students of the First Grade*. On the day of the film, everyone lined up and walked to the Beijing Normal University auditorium. In addition to the students from Beishi Erxiao, students from Number One Primary School also came to watch the movie. It was a black-and-white film, and the main character in it was a little girl called Malyusha.

The movie was fascinating. It told the story of Malyusha's life – her happiness, troubles, excitement and fun. In addition, she also praised her teacher, Anna Ivanovna, who was an amiable and lovely person.

That movie made Little Auspicious feel very kind. Like his classmates, he wished that Malyusha could be in his class. Watching the teachers in the film, the students in Little Auspicious's class couldn't help but think of their teacher, Ms Guan Qi, who was sitting behind them.

The students were unaware, but their parents knew of Ms Guan Qi's fame. She was known as one of the country's top teachers and was considered a model worker. On the first day of school, Little Auspicious knew from his mother's delighted eyes when she saw Ms Guan that he had an amiable and lovely teacher.

Little Auspicious liked listening most of all to the last three minutes of Ms Guan's lessons. Usually, she would finish the class ahead of time and then say, 'Today's class is over, and there are three minutes to go. Now I will tell you some fun trivia.'

The students would solemnly put their books and notebooks together and put their hands behind their backs as if they could only use their ears. Little Auspicious sometimes thought that even if the books and notebooks were not closed, it would not hinder their listening. But everyone did it like a ritual, and no one dared break it.

One day after Chinese class, Ms Guan said, 'Students, please raise your hands.' No one knew exactly what she meant, so most students raised one hand and looked to the left and right. Ms Guan asked again, 'How many hands do each of us have?'

'Two!' they all said together.

'Last time I told you the difference between the left hand and the right hand. Now, everyone, raise both hands in front of your eyes. Today, we are going to take a closer look at the fingers of our two hands. The first joint...' Ms Guan raised her hands to her eyes.

'What did you see?' Ms Guan asked.

'I saw the meat.' Pu Yunsheng, a boy sitting in the last row, would give a silly answer like that every time. Sure enough, everyone laughed.

'Big Brother, Second Thumb Brother, Bell and Drum Tower (singing big operas), Huguo Temple, Little Niuniu...'

The students stretched their fingers and began to talk.

(Little Auspicious never understood why the ring finger was called 'Huguo Temple'. He once asked his father, who told him that maybe it was because 'Si' ('temple') and 'Si' ('four') had the same pronunciation. In front of it is the Bell and Drum Tower

(Zhong Gu Lou); take a 'middle' (Zhong) pun, and then take a 'four', making it easy to remember.)

Ms Guan said with a smile, 'There are circular patterns on the skin of the fingertips. Do you see them?'

'I see!' everyone answered in unison.

'That's what fingerprints are, and everyone's fingerprints are different from everyone else's.'

The students became interested and began to look curiously at each other's fingertips.

Ms Guan said, 'Everyone's own fingerprints are not all the same. One is called a "bucket", and the other is called a "dust-pan". Some people have one bucket, and the rest are dustpans. Some people have two buckets, and the rest are dustpans... Eight dustpans.'

Everyone began to count their dustpans.

Pu Yunsheng spoke again. 'Teacher, which is better, having more buckets or more dustpans?'

Ms Guan shook her head. 'There is no distinction between good and bad in this. In the same way that people's faces are different, fingerprints can be used to identify people. People are not good or bad according to their appearance, but by their morality.'

Back home, Little Auspicious and his father talked about the school. His father took out a newspaper and said, 'Ms Gu-an has been mentioned in the newspaper.'

Little Auspicious took the newspaper and saw three itali-cised characters: 'Listening to Classes'. It was an article about Teacher Guan Qi. Little Auspicious remembered those three words: Listening to Classes.

The students noticed that when she was in class, Ms Gu-an had wet patches on her chest. They later learned that these were the traces left by her milk. Some of the students even saw

Ms Guan expressing her milk into a cup in the office. Little Auspicious was very curious.

When he got home, he quietly told his mother about the mysterious thing about Ms Guan. His mother said that Ms Guan was breastfeeding her child, and some mothers produce so much milk that it can leak out by itself.

Little Auspicious widened his eyes.

In his mind, Ms Guan was so respectable. How could she still breastfeed her child like an ordinary housewife? He couldn't imagine Ms Guan nursing a baby.

How could she be like an ordinary person? Little Auspicious could never figure that out.

CHAPTER NINE

Lao Dezi at the Opposite Door

Opposite the door of Little Auspicious's house was a small courtyard. When entering the door, there was a big 'Fu' ('Fortune') character carved into the brick. There was a courtyard to the east of the character Fu, and Uncle Dong lived in the side house. There was a smaller side house to the west of the character Fu, in which lived Uncle Guo, who was of the same generation as Little Auspicious's father in terms of seniority. They were older than his father, so Little Auspicious called them great uncles.

Uncle Dong had a son who was in his fifties. Little Auspicious called him 'Brother Dong'. Brother Dong had eight children. Uncle Dong had a second son, whom Little Auspicious called 'Second Brother Dong'. The second brother had four children in his family. Uncle Dong also had a young son the same age as Big Auspicious, and the two boys often played together.

Little Auspicious's father told him that the original Dong family had consisted only of Uncle Dong and Aunt Dong. Now there were more than ten people.

Uncle Guo and Aunt Guo, in the west courtyard, had eleven children. Among the eleven children was a boy named Guo

Deping who was the same age as Little Auspicious. All thirteen people in Uncle Guo's family lived in two north rooms and a small south room.

Guo Deping was Little Auspicious's good friend. They were the same age, and they would often visit each other. Little Auspicious had a nickname among the neighbours – 'Big Talk Auspicious's – and Guo Deping had a similar one: 'Big Mouth Guo'. Guo Deping was given his nickname because he would always tell people that his house had a small garden and a small bridge, but, in fact, his yard didn't even have a tree. Big Mouth Guo got his name from boasting too much.

Little Auspicious called Guo Deping 'Lao Dezi'.

Sometimes, Lao Dezi would stay at Little Auspicious's house for the whole day, leaving only when it was time to eat. At that time, a meal was a big deal, so the children all understood this rule. No matter how good someone else's meal was, no matter how greedy or hungry they were, they had to leave to avoid embarrassing others.

One day, Little Auspicious's family made dumplings. The dumplings had already been placed on the plate, but Lao Dezi had yet to leave. Little Auspicious's mother told him to eat, but he refused. Little Auspicious knew that Lao Dezi wanted to eat them very much, but he was embarrassed. He felt that Lao Dezi had been too slow to react. If he had not intended to eat, he should have just left. When his mother asked again, Lao Dezi ate one dumpling and then took a look at Little Auspicious. Little Auspicious didn't speak but looked the other way. Lao Dezi stood up and walked out. Little Auspicious watched him as he left and felt a little regretful.

Because Lao Dezi's family had many children, life for them was more difficult than for Little Auspicious's family. There was a rural stove at the door of the south house. This kind of stove was usually only seen in rural areas or used temporarily for cooking during marches and wars. There was a large pot on the stove, much larger than ordinary pots. Their family's meals were cooked there.

Mealtime at their house was often reminiscent of a big dining hall. Eating too much or not enough was often the reason for quarrels amongst the children. Aunt Guo had her own unique way of managing the family's meals. She distributed equal shares of food among them, just like in a cafeteria.

It was easy to cook premade meals, but on some days, the children would take the raw materials and cook what they wanted for themselves. There was just one stove; therefore, they would have to cook one after the other.

Little Auspicious happened to be at their house at noon on one such day. Aunt Guo weighed out three *tael*s (150 grams) of stick noodles for everyone. Some of the children made stick noodle porridge to save time, and some made dough drop soup. Lao Dezi mixed in extra water to soften the dough, then formed three small pancakes and put them in the pot, covering it with a lid.

Little Auspicious looked at him in surprise and asked, 'Will it work?' Lao Dezi nodded.

After about twenty minutes, Little Auspicious smelt a fragrant aroma. Lao Dezi uncovered the pot and used a spatula to take out the pancakes. Yellow spots had formed on the undersides of the pancakes.

'Do you want one?' he asked, holding up a small pancake.

'Is it cooked?' Little Auspicious asked.

'It's cooked!' Lao Dezi handed the pancake to Little Auspicious. He took a bite. He hadn't expected it to be so sweet. Lao Dezi said, 'Pancakes made in a big firewood pot are delicious!'

When he got home, Little Auspicious told his mother that he had gone to Lao Dezi's house to eat pancakes. My mother said, 'Look at Lao Dezi! The other day he ate one of our dumplings, and you screwed up your face at him.'

Little Auspicious said, 'I didn't stop him from eating!'

His mother shook her head. 'It's not good to look at people like that. I didn't say anything to you that day, but I am telling you today that you must be kind.'

Little Auspicious stopped talking, because his mother was right.

CHAPTER TEN

Xizhimen

Little Auspicious's home was only a quarter of an hour from Xizhimen (an area around the West Gate). He knew it well before he became a primary school student. On his way to school each day, Little Auspicious would get his first glimpse of Xizhimen when he came out of Nancaochang Street.

At Xizhimen, a large tower rose above the gate through the bluish-grey city wall. It perched on the wall like an old man sitting after having travelled for thousands of years and through the vicissitudes of life. The tower seemed to be breathing, as if alive.

On the city side of the wall, one could ascend to the top of the wall along the horse path next to the city gate. In its disrepair, many potholes had formed in the brick paving. There were jujube branches poking through along the city wall, with small jujubes on them. Picking jujubes was a big temptation for many children, and their clothes would get ripped and their arms scratched as they climbed to pick them. On top of the city wall, one could look into the distance and see the horizon connecting sky and earth.

At that time, the areas separated by the city wall were two different worlds. Upon leaving the city gate, there were very few houses to be seen. There were only unpaved roads and fields full of crops. There were also fewer pedestrians, carriages and horses on the road, and only occasionally could a few houses and temples be seen by the roadside. Travellers entering this landscape from the city suddenly felt smaller, and there was a sense of lifelessness.

Uncle Dong, from the opposite house, liked the children very much, and the children liked to run to his house. Uncle Dong had a radio, and he was a good storyteller. But, peculiarly, he wouldn't tell stories to just one or two children; he would only tell stories if there were at least three children. Therefore, if Little Auspicious wanted to listen to a story, he had to organise the audience, and the first one he would call was Lao Dezi: 'Lao Dezi! Come hear a story!'

Lao Dezi always came when he was called. Then Little Auspicious would shout in the yard, 'Uncle Dong is telling a story!'

One day when he was telling a story, Uncle Dong talked about Xizhimen again. 'The Gaoliang Bridge is outside of Xizhimen, have you heard of it?' Little Auspicious and Lao Dezi quickly said, 'I know! I know!'

Uncle Dong started his story:

> According to legend, in the Ming Dynasty, one day, Prime Minister Liu Bowen found Gao Liang, his beloved general, and handed him a sharp silver spear, saying, 'You will wait outside Xizhimen tomorrow morning. When the gate opens, an old man and his wife will come out pushing a wheelbarrow, and there will be two wooden barrels, one on the left and one on the right. Go up; don't say anything; just pierce the barrels with your spear and run away. Don't look back, no matter how much they yell at you.'
>
> 'Why should I stab someone's barrel for no reason?' Gao Liang asked.

'The secret must not be leaked,' Liu Bowen said calmly.

That night, Gao Liang waited outside Xizhimen. At dawn, the city gate opened.

'Zhi Yo Yo, Zhi Yo Yo.' An old man pushed a wheelbarrow out of the city gate, followed by an old lady. Gao Liang walked over and, without further ado, raised his silver spear and stabbed them one at a time, piercing the two barrels. He turned and ran away, only to hear the old man shouting from behind, 'Young man, why did you pierce my barrels?' Gao Liang didn't dare to turn his head and ran; he heard the sound of roaring waves coming from behind. But Gao Liang couldn't help it; he looked back. Gao Liang was drowned by a huge wave that swept across the sky.

It turned out that the old man was the Dragon King of the North Sea, and his wife was the Dragon Po. They wanted to steal all the water in Beijing so that the people of Beijing would die of thirst. The water in those two barrels was almost all the water in Beijing. When Gao Liang had punctured the barrels, the water had returned to Beijing again. To commemorate Gao Liang, the Gao Liang Bridge was erected outside Xizhimen.

After Uncle Dong finished the story, Little Auspicious asked, 'Why did the Dragon King take the water from Beijing?'

Uncle Dong smiled slightly, 'Now, that's a story for another time!'

'Grandpa, tell us a ghost story – the scary one!' said Uncle Dong's grandson Xiaochong. By now, the sky was getting dark, and several more children gathered around Uncle Dong. Uncle Dong lit his pipe, coughed and said, 'I will tell you a ghost story that is not scary...'

The yard was quiet for a moment, except for the sound of crickets.

Uncle Dong said:

Xizhimen, during the Ming and Qing dynasties, was the gate through which water delivered from Yuquan Mountain to the Imperial Palace had to pass; hence the name 'Water Gate'.

Where there is a city wall, there is a moat, and the moat at that time was still very large. Every year, people would drown in it.

When he said this, some of the children couldn't help but look around and huddle together.

Outside Xizhimen, there was an old man selling baked sweet potatoes near the base of the city wall. In his small house, the sound of water from the moat could be heard.

One voice said, 'Brother, I'm leaving tomorrow. I've had enough of the sins here.'

Another voice questioned, 'How do you have such good luck?'

The first voice replied, 'Someone is coming to take my place tomorrow.'

'Who is it?'

'A fat man in a grey coat. Come over as soon as the city gate opens. Don't tell anyone else!'

The old man was shocked. He knew that he had heard two water ghosts talking. Someone would drown tomorrow morning and become a new water ghost, and the one of the existing water ghosts would go away.

'Battah', 'Battah.' The two walked towards the river again. Then there was a sound of water, 'Hualala', 'Hualala.' After that, it went quiet.

The next day, just after dawn, before the city gate opened, the old man was waiting outside the gate. As soon as the gate opened, he stared wide-eyed to see if a fat man in a grey coat would come out. Before quarter of an hour had passed, a tall, fat man walked through the gate. He wore a new-looking grey coat. The old man followed behind him without saying a word.

The man in the grey coat went straight towards the river. The old man followed closely, then caught up to him and asked, 'Sir, where are you going?'

The man in the grey coat was in a stupor, and he continued walking towards the river without answering. The old man hid his surprise and overtook the man in the grey coat. He turned around and stood in front of him, then he stretched out his hand and slapped the man! The man was stunned and looked at the water in front of him in surprise, as if he had just woken up. 'Oh! Where am I?'

'If you go any further, you will fall into the river!' said the old man.

The fat man woke up as, if from a dream, and clasped his hands, 'Thank you, sir! What's the matter with me? Am I seeking death?' After speaking, he left in gratitude. The old man breathed a sigh of relief.

Unexpectedly, the water ghost came out of the river that night, dragging a large puddle of river mud to the old man's window, and he cursed him: 'You old bastard! You meddled and ruined my business. I'm not finished with you!'

These stories were very strange. Little Auspicious remembered them all. One day, the teacher asked the students to tell a story, and Little Auspicious told the story of the uncle who baked sweet potatoes, and his classmate Bian Yu told the story of Gao Liang catching the water. Bian Yu was praised by the teacher. The teacher didn't say anything about Little Auspicious's story. Little Auspicious didn't dare ask why. After thinking about it for a long time, it may have been because Bian Yu had told a story about gods, while Little Auspicious had told a story about ghosts.

Later, Little Auspicious concluded that although ghost stories were exciting, they could only be told in private. In contrast, stories about gods could be told in class.

Little Auspicious asked his mother who the good guy was in the story of the water ghost, and his mother said that the baked sweet potato seller had a good heart, as he had wanted to save someone's life.

At that time, the city gates of Beijing were closed every evening, including Xizhimen. One day, Little Auspicious's older brother went to play outside the city, but when he arrived at Xizhimen to return home, the gate had just closed. He and his companions ran quickly south along the city wall. To the south was Fucheng Gate, which they knew closed half an hour later than the gate at Xizhimen. When they arrived at Fucheng Gate, the city gate was halfway closed. They yelled and ran faster and managed to get in just before the gates closed. If they had not made it in through the gate, they would have been unable to go home that day.

CHAPTER ELEVEN

New Friend

The newcomer in the front yard was an old gentleman, a university professor. His surname was Lao, meaning 'old'. So, when Little Auspicious called him Mr Lao, it had two meanings.

The Lao family had moved from Zhongnanhai. In the early days of the founding of New China, some civilians still lived in Zhongnanhai, and there was a middle school named Sicun Middle School.

Later, Zhongnanhai became the seat of the Central People's Government, so the Lao family moved out. Sicun Middle School moved to Fuxue Alley and merged with Beiping Number Eight Middle School, which was renamed Beijing Number Eight Middle School. Another middle school, Chengda Middle School, beside Zhongshan Park, was later renamed Number Twenty-Eight Middle School.

Mr Lao had two daughters. The eldest was called Elder Ms Lao, and the second daughter was called Second Ms Lao. Every time Little Auspicious called their names, it felt strange, because their surname was very rare.

Mr Lao's daughters were both graduates of art colleges, where they had learnt painting. In Mr Lao's room, an oil portrait of him painted by the Elder Ms Lao hung above the second door. Mr Lao was thin, but he had been depicted even thinner in the painting. Why had he been depicted so thin? Little Auspicious was puzzled by this.

The Second Ms Lao had a son who was a little younger than Little Auspicious. His name was Xiaotian. The arrival of Xiaotian made Little Auspicious happy. Xiaotian became Little Auspicious's good friend.

Xiaotian's father's name was Zhu You. This name was pronounced exactly the same as the word for 'pork' in the Shandong dialect, especially when said with a Jiaodong accent. Whenever Little Auspicious thought of his name, he could not help but laugh. Fortunately for him, Little Auspicious remembered to address him as 'Uncle Zhu' or 'Mr Zhu' every time.

Uncle Zhu was a very amicable and easy-going person. He dressed casually and was tall and burly, with a deep and charming voice. Uncle Zhu would smoke a pipe occasionally. His shredded tobacco smelt very fragrant to Little Auspicious.

When Uncle Zhu took Xiaotian out to play, they would often take Little Auspicious with them. Once, they went to play table tennis at a club west of Beihai Park Lake. It was the first time Little Auspicious saw a real table tennis table.

A few days later, something happened to Little Auspicious that made him appreciate Uncle Zhu even more. Shortly after three o'clock one afternoon, when Little Auspicious entered the courtyard gate after returning from school, he saw Xiaotian playing alone beside the rockery. When Xiaotian saw Little Auspicious, he said, 'Let's play for a while.'

'What are we going play?'

Xiaotian pointed to an opening in the ground of the front yard and asked Little Auspicious, 'What is this?'

There were two rectangular openings under the corridor of the north house, one of which was covered by a pane of glass. The other pane had been removed and placed on the grass beside the opening. Little Auspicious had seen it every day and had become used to it. So he replied, 'This is the entrance to the basement.'

'What is inside?'

'I don't know.'

'Have you ever gone in?'

'No.' Little Auspicious told the truth.

'Coward!'

'If you aren't scared, then *you* go in.'

'Your father's the landlord, and my father is the tenant. *You* have to go in first.'

'How about we go in together?' Little Auspicious put his schoolbag aside. He had always wanted to see what was inside there. Xiaotian's curiosity strengthened his courage.

'Okay, you go in first. I'll follow you,' Xiaotian stated.

Walking around a tall rose bush, Little Auspicious picked up a foot-long stick, and then climbed down into the hole with Xiaotian following behind.

The basement ceiling was shallow. As they kneeled in the space, their heads touched the ceiling, so they crouched lower and crawled forward.

'Are you afraid of cats?' Little Auspicious asked.

'I'm not afraid of cats; I'm afraid of cats scratching me. Are you scared?' Xiaotian countered bravely.

Little Auspicious said, 'I'm not afraid of cats. I'm afraid of mice.'

As they moved forward, it got darker and darker. The only light came from the opening behind them. Little Auspicious turned around a corner, and the space behind it was pitch black. Little Auspicious knocked on the ceiling above his head. It was wooden.

'Xiaotian!'

No answer. He suddenly felt panic.

'Xiaotian!'

Xiaotian answered, his voice trembling. 'I saw a mouse!'

'Really? Did it run away?'

'No, it's still staring at me!'

Little Auspicious suddenly felt his scalp go numb, and his whole body was covered with goosebumps. He didn't move.

'I'm a little scared... How about you?' Xiaotian said.

'Me too. Let's get out.'

'Okay,' Xiaotian said.

'Is the mouse still there?'

'Looks like it's still there – right by the entrance!'

As they said that, they retreated backwards. When they were about to leave the basement, Little Auspicious gritted his teeth and looked arround. Sure enough, there was something shining with a mischievous glint looking back at him. Little Auspicious waved the stick and shouted boldly, 'I'm not afraid of you!'

The thing didn't move at all. Little Auspicious poked forward with the stick. The stick touched something the size of a fist, but it still didn't move. Little Auspicious trembled as he reached forward and picked up the 'mouse'. It felt too heavy to be a mouse. He took it in his hand and climbed up out of the basement.

When he stood up, Xiaotian was already standing there. But he didn't expect to see the two adults standing in front of him – Xiaotian's father and Little Auspicious's mother. They looked very serious, and Little Auspicious became nervous.

Mother said, 'Who let you in?'

'He let me in.' Little Auspicious pointed to Xiaotian.

'Are you older, or is he older?'

'I'm older.' Little Auspicious lowered his head and glanced at Xiaotian.

'You are older and must set an example for the little ones. What if there was a hole in it? What if you got hurt? What if a stray cat scratched you? Your father said a long time ago that, in this courtyard, you weren't allowed to climb the rockery or crawl into the basement.' The more his mother talked, the angrier she became.

Uncle Zhu smiled, and he said to Little Auspicious's mother, 'Mrs Auspicious, don't be angry. It's good for these two boys to be curious, even if it's an adventure. I don't think there's any danger in this basement. Just dust each other off.' He pulled Little Auspicious over, brushed his clothes, and smiled as if nothing had happened.

Little Auspicious and Xiaotian laughed while brushing off their clothes, and, unexpectedly, Little Auspicious's mother laughed, too.

His mother saw that he was holding something. 'What's in your hand?'

Little Auspicious handed it over with both hands. 'I don't know what this is. Xiaotian thought it was a mouse.'

Xiaotian said, 'That is definitely not what I saw!'

Little Auspicious's mother took it in her hand and said, 'It looks like iron that has been smashed and flattened. It's so dirty. Throw it away!'

Uncle Zhu took it and tried to bend it with his hands.

Little Auspicious said, 'I will sell it to someone who collects scrap metal so that I can buy a few pieces of candy to eat!'

Everyone returned to their homes. Little Auspicious thought that he was fortunate to have met Uncle Zhu that day.

At night, Little Auspicious showed his father the lump of iron he had found in the basement. His father examined it and said, 'It looks like a big smoke lamp that has been smashed flat. It's made of silver.'

'What is a smoke lamp?'

'In the old society, some people didn't know better, and they smoked opium. They had to have this thing when they smoked. Now the country strictly prohibits smoking opium, and no one dares to smoke it anymore.'

Several days later, his father told him, 'You didn't explore in vain. The thing you picked up sold for one yuan.'

His father had taken it to the market and sold it.

'Why was it so valuable?'

'It was based on the price of scrap silver,' said his father.

'Ah!' Little Auspicious was very happy.

'How do you want to spend it?'

Little Auspicious thought for a while. 'Let's keep it and spend it on our daily essentials.'

His father's lips moved, but he didn't speak. He just touched Little Auspicious's face gently and walked away.

CHAPTER TWELVE

Mr Lao and the Elder Ms Lao

Mr Lao was very capable. He prepared blueprints for inventions and then had his workers make samples for him. He was also a consultant to many factories.

The living room where Sachiko had lived had been turned into a metalworking workshop – essentially an inventor's workshop – which housed several machine tools. The two or three people who worked there served Mr Lao's inventing and manufacturing processes. Mr Lao often spent time working there himself.

What excited Little Auspicious the most was that Mr Lao would make toys and models.

One day, Mr Lao asked Little Auspicious and several other children to look at a 'little machine' he had made. It was a very delicate model of a briquette assembly line. The whole thing was only about the size of a drawer. *Although the sparrow is small, it has all its five internal organs.* The parts were miniature but functional, every gear and lever shining with a blue lustre.

What was even more impressive was that the machine started to move when the power was turned on. Little Auspicious was stunned. Was this a machine or a toy?

Mr Lao put black coal powder into the hopper on the left with his bony hands, and when he pressed the switch, the machine would automatically fill with water and stir, turning the coal powder into small coal balls the size of pigeon eggs. Then, they were put into moulds the size of bottle caps and were shaped into small round cakes. They moved along the assembly line like small black pastries. Finally, another mould with twelve needles moved down, drilling twelve holes in the small round cakes. When miniature briquettes came off the conveyor belt, Little Auspicious was dumbfounded.

Mr Lao was a southerner who spoke Cantonese. Little Auspicious couldn't understand half of what he said, but he could guess what he was going to do from his facial expressions and movements. Mr Lao was he was short and very thin. To Little Auspicious, it seemed as if he always hunched his body and walked like a chicken pecking at rice – bowing and bowing. His strength was not his body but his bespectacled head.

One day, when Little Auspicious came home from school, the Elder Ms Lao was cleaning her goldfish bowl. Since they had moved here, many flowers and plants that Little Auspicious had never seen before had been added to the lawn in the front yard, as were two fishponds, each one metre in diameter. The goldfish in them added vitality to the yard. Unfortunately, crows and magpies wanted to eat the fish, so the Elder Ms Lao got some bamboo sticks and stuck them in the mud at the bottom of the ponds. The bamboo sticks were densely packed so that the birds couldn't get near the water, and the fish were safe.

'The student is back!" The Elder Ms Lao greeted Little Auspicious with a smile.

'Yes, I'm back!'

'Which school do you go to?'

'Beishi Erxiao.'

'Hey, that's great! Come, Little Auspicious, sing *Little Son-in-law* for us.' The Elder Ms Lao took his hand. Whenever she saw him, she would always ask him to sing *Little Son-in-law*. The Elder Ms Lao was not tall, and she walked in a hurry. Although she was alone, she always used 'We' to refer to herself.

'Sing a song!' His mother came over. She thought that it was a great way to thank someone for their greeting.

Little Auspicious sang, 'Birds enter the forest, chickens nest, it's dark – the sky, Yang Xiangcao guards the lonely lamp, in a dilemma... In my heart, there are so many things...'

Little Son-in-Law was a Pingju opera. Little Auspicious remembered going with his mother to watch it at the theatre. He clearly remembered that on the stage, a toddler was lying on the bed and sleeping. A mother in her twenties named Yang Xiangcao went to a window and closed it. As the lights on the stage gradually began to dime, Yang Xiangcao lit a small oil lamp and began to babble and sing. Halfway through the song, the child on the bed cried out, "Mom, I want to pee!" But Yang Xiangcao was not his mother but his wife. The child fell asleep after peeing in the potty.

Yang Xiangcao started to sing again. Little Auspicious remembered feeling that Yang Xiangcao was very pitiful.

The song in this section of the opera was very long, but Little Auspicious could sing it perfectly. The Elder Ms Lao listened intently as he sang. Apart from when she listened to *Little Son-in-Law*, she never showed such an expression. By the end, her eyes were watery. Little Auspicious thought she was upset, so he paused. But she grabbed his hand and said, 'Sing!'

Little Auspicious continued to sing. He couldn't remember how many times he had sung *Little Son-in-law* to the Elder Ms Lao. Today was just one of many times.

One time, Little Auspicious had felt tired and suggested, 'Let me sing *Liu Qiaoer* for you!' But the Elder Ms Lao had shaken her head and said, with a smile, 'Sing *Little Son-in-law* first, and then sing other songs later.'

Every time he sang *Little Son-in-Law*, the Elder Ms Lao would kiss him on the cheek. Little Auspicious didn't like her kissing him like this, but there was nothing he could do. As soon as he finished *Little Son-in-law*, she would let him go. She didn't seem interested in *Liu Qiaoer*.

'Elder Ms Lao' was what older people called her. Children were not allowed to call her that. Little Auspicious's mother told him that she should be addressed as 'Elder Aunt'. Little Auspicious found it was easier to say the three words, though, and would frequently forget and accidentally call her 'Elder Ms Lao' in person.

Although Elder Ms Lao was not old, nor was she young. She was a veritable old maid, so the word 'Elder' in this case had multiple meanings.

There were many interesting things in Mr Lao's house. There was a thin glass duck, as tall as a pencil, mounted on a stand. There was a small basin of water in front of the duck, and the duck would sway backwards and forwards. Its beak would get closer and closer to the water, until, finally, its beak would touch the water. Then the duck would lift out of the basin and swing back up again, starting the cycle over again, repeatedly, never-endingly.

Seeing Little Auspicious's dumbfounded look, Mr Lao told him that the glass duck contained a chemical called ether, a liquid that evaporated easily. When the ether at the bottom of the duck evaporated and filled the duck's head, the duck's head would gradually become heavier, causing the duck's head to sway lower and lower. Then, when the head touched the water,

the ether would cool and it flow back down to the base of the duck, making the duck's head lighter, and causing it to sway less deeply, until the ether evaporated again…

This kind of explanation Little Auspicious could understand!

There were many books and magazines in the Laos' house, such as *Little Friends*, *Children's Times* and *Pictorials*. Little Auspicious spent much time reading magazines at their house.

The Second Ms Lao was very strict with Xiaotian. One day, she told Xiaotian to take a small folding stool and sit in front of the goldfish bowl to paint. It was embarrassing for Little Auspicious when he came to ask to play with Xiaotian.

'Xiaotian is painting. You can play later!' said the Second Ms Lao.

'How long?' Little Auspicious asked without being aware of the situation.

'When Xiaotian finishes his painting, I'll let him find you.'

Little Auspicious went home unhappy. Even when it was almost time for dinner, Xiaotian still hadn't come to look for him. Little Auspicious ran to the front yard and saw that Xiaotian was gone.

Little Auspicious's sister told him that if people didn't come to him, that meant that they didn't want to play with him. 'Don't beg for anything. How shameless!' When she said this, he became very angry. 'Why did Xiaotian's mother lie to me? I will never play with him again! I won't even wait at the door of his house!'

However, a few days later, Xiaotian came to the door. It was noon. Little Auspicious had been napping. When he woke, he saw a shadow on the window to the corridor. It was Xiaotian! But before Little Auspicious could stand up, the figure outside the window had disappeared.

Sometimes it was hard to play together. One day, Little Auspicious's mother told him, 'Don't stay in other people's homes all the time. They may have other things to do and might feel embarrassed to tell you.'

'They're fine.' Little Auspicious said.

His mother turned him around and said seriously, 'Why do the Laos let you sit in their home for a long time? Why did they take you to visit the toy exhibition? This is not their responsibility. They treat you very well, but you have to appreciate what others do for you.'

Little Auspicious listened and lowered his head silently.

CHAPTER THIRTEEN

The Milky White Tree

One day, Little Auspicious went to Mr Lao's house to play again. He saw a strange little toy tree on a desk. The small tree was made of a piece of milky white oak the size of a teacup. The white oak was cut with a knife so that the still-connected shavings curled up to form a shape resembling an umbrella.

The little tree fascinated him deeply. He liked it very much, and he didn't want to let it go. Seeing there was no one in the room, he quietly put the little tree into his pocket, even though he knew that it was bad to take other people's things.

At dusk the next day, while his mother was doing needlework in the corner of the room, Little Auspicious was playing a military game he had invented. The broom for sweeping the bed was on the table denoting a camp. The bristles of the broom were the forest and a drapery cloth served as high mountains. The soldiers on one side were represented with white Go (a board game) pieces, and the soldiers on the other side with black Go pieces.

There was a knock on the door. It was the Elder Ms Lao.

Little Auspicious hurried to hide in the shed where the sundries were stored, straining his ears to listen to their conversation. Then, he remembered that he had stolen the toy tree the day before, and it was in a little box under his bed. He was a little scared, and he didn't dare come out. He couldn't hear what the Elder Ms Lao and his mother were saying. He waited in fear.

He heard his mother call for him, 'Come on, Auntie has brought you toys.'

Little Auspicious walked into the room hesitantly. He didn't understand what his mother was talking about.

Elder Ms Lao was sitting on a chair. She smiled at him. On the table were a beige wind-up chicken made of tin and a black machine gun made of bamboo, both brand new. Following a sign from his mother, he hurriedly expressed his thanks to the Elder Ms Lao.

At that moment, he had completely forgotten about having taken the small tree.

When the Elder Ms Lao left, Little Auspicious picked up the machine gun and twisted the handle. It made a crisp clicking sound. He saw that his mother was watching him and suddenly remembered that the Elder Ms Lao had said something before he had come into the room. So he anxiously put the machine gun on the table and waited for the storm. Unexpectedly, his mother just said, lovingly, 'Go and play in the yard. You are too noisy inside.'

During dinner, Little Auspicious's mother said to his father, 'It's not a new year or a festival. But Elder Ms Lao gave Little Auspicious a toy. Why do you think that was?'

His father looked at Little Auspicious, 'Did you ask someone for something?'

Little Auspicious shook his head.

That night, he didn't sleep well. He didn't understand the connection between his receiving toys and stealing the little tree, but he knew that he had made a big mistake, and he wanted to return it. The next day, he quietly took out the tree. His dirty hands had blackened the leaves. He washed them with soap for a long time, but they were still dirty. Not only were they not clean, but they had also become darker after being washed.

After he had woken up from a nap at noon, his mother asked him, 'Is there anything you didn't tell me?'

Little Auspicious shook his head automatically, but he knew that his mother suspected something.

'Did you do anything wrong?'

Then Little Auspicious offered no further resistance and told his mother the whole story.

His mother's face became serious. 'This is very serious, you know.'

'I know.' Little Auspicious lowered his head.

'Are you going to talk to her yourself, or should I take you to talk to her?'

'I'll go by myself,' Little Auspicious cried.

'Do you know what to say?'

'"I took things from your home. I was wrong, and I will never dare to do it again."'

When it was time for dinner that day, Little Auspicious stood in the front yard at the door of the living room, waiting. He didn't have the courage to knock on the door.

After a long time, he finally raised his hand to knock. But before he could, the door opened, and Mr Lao came out. He was surprised to see Little Auspicious. 'Is there anything wrong? Come back tomorrow. We have to go out.'

'I'm looking for Elder Ms Lao.'

Elder Ms Lao appeared behind him. It looked as if she was about to go out on a date. Little Auspicious couldn't bear it anymore. He couldn't wait until tomorrow. He took out a handkerchief from his pocket and opened it, revealing the small pine tree, 'Auntie, I took something from your house. I made a mistake and won't dare to repeat it.'

Mr Lao lowered his head slightly and looked over his glasses as if to ask, 'What's going on?'

Elder Ms Lao smiled and said, 'I gave this little tree to Little Auspicious to play with, and now he has brought it back. Ah, it's a little dirty. No worries. You can go home now.'

Little Auspicious was stunned for a moment. Had the Elder Ms Lao not heard his apology?

Elder Ms Lao helped Mr Lao down the steps.

Three days later, Little Auspicious again saw the small tree in the old man's living room, once again beautiful and milky white.

'How did you clean it?' he asked.

Mr Lao shook his head and said, 'I made it again.'

'Where is the dirty one?'

Mr Lao opened the drawer and took out a small tree, which was emerald green with shiny varnish on it. The two trees, one white and the other green, were vivid and lovely!

CHAPTER FOURTEEN

The Small Black Date Chen Yanping

The students all hoped that Ms Guan would like them. And, indeed, Ms Guan did say that she liked them all. Two months passed, and Teacher Guan became familiar with the students, and the students were also familiar with each other. Everyone thought that Ms Guan's favourite in the class was Chen Yanping.

After class, many of the students surrounded Ms Guan. They couldn't help tugging at the hem of her clothes and sometimes called her 'Mother' by mistake.

Little Auspicious thought it was ridiculous and felt that those children were immature. How could they not be able to tell the difference between their own mothers and Ms Guan? But Little Auspicious especially hoped that she would touch his head. He recalled that she had only touched his head twice this semester. Ms Guan liked to touch Chen Yanping's head the most. In Little Auspicious's eyes, she almost always put her hands on Chen Yanping's head.

Chen Yanping was the shortest and thinnest in the class. He sat in the first row, directly across from the teacher's desk.

On the day of registration, when Little Auspicious and his mother were looking at the admission list on the wall, a boy's voice had come from behind, asking, 'Are you going to this primary school?' Little Auspicious recalled looking back and seeing a thin, small boy with a dark complexion. He looked like a small black date. His eyes were black and very round, like those of a mouse, and they looked very energetic. Little Auspicious could easily remember him.

Ms Guan liked Chen Yanping the most because, although his family's life was very difficult, his academic performance was the best in the class, and he was kind and disciplined.

Chen Yanping was also well known among the parents, who would often tell their children to learn from Chen Yanping.

One day, when everyone was playing pinball, Pu Yunsheng blurted out, 'Chen Yanping doesn't have a father!' The students who heard this were stunned for a moment.

Little Auspicious had been to Chen Yanping's home. His home was very small. The space was like a hallway, and it could accommodate only a bed and a small table. His mother was a tailor; she sewed people's clothes for a living. Like Chen Yanping, his mother was also very dark and thin. She wore two long braids, which didn't make her look younger; instead, they made her look older. Her eyes, as bright as black lacquer, were unforgettable for Little Auspicious.

The temptations on the way to school were great.

Dacheng Alley exited onto Nancaochang Street less than fifty metres away from the school, but lining the street were food stalls that fascinated the students – every three steps, there was another stall to look at; every five steps, there was something to stop for. The first stall was on a high step. It sold snacks and knick-knacks. Little Auspicious was most interested in two things: silly-cake and honey-stick. The silly-cake was no bigger than Little Auspicious's fist. It was made by putting boiled hawthorn paste into a small bowl of glutinous rice. People ate it with a small wooden spoon. The honey-stick was a green apricot that had been skewered on a sorghum straw stick and then dipped in a bowl of white sugar syrup. Instead of biting the honey-stick, it was better to lick it. The price for each of these treats was two cents.

Further along the street was a crossroads, with a barber shop on one corner and a biscuit shop on the other. The biscuit shop sold sesame seed cakes for three cents each, and fried ghosts (a kind of churro) cost two cents. Also for sale were tofu soup and soy milk. Little Auspicious and most of his classmates seldom went in because they couldn't afford such a 'luxury' breakfast. On the northeast corner was a fruit stand where were only two things that Little Auspicious could afford. One was fruit peels. The peels, left over from making canned fruit, had been soaked in sugar water and then dried and placed in a basket on the counter. Fruit peels were much cheaper than fruit. The other was jujube stones. Gualuo jujubes, a popular snack in Beijing, were prepared by removing the pits by machine and then drying the fruit to produce Gualuo dates. The remaining jujube stones still had a small amount of edible flesh on them. These stones were also dried and were sold at the fruit stand as treats for children, who would eat them like a puppy chewing on a bone.

One day, Ms Guan talked in the class meeting about eating snacks. She told everyone that snacking was bad. If one got into the habit of eating snacks, one wouldn't be able to save money; and, also, eating snacks was unhygienic. She also pointed to two sisters in the class, Cui Keqin and Cui Kejian, and said that the children should all behave in the way that their names suggested: Keqin ('moderately diligent') and Kejian ('moderately austere'). Finally, she praised Chen Yanping, saying that he never ate snacks.

理髮店
烧餅

'Teacher, there is a problem!' Liu Guangting spoke while raising his hands. Ms Guan just glanced at him. He realised that he had spoken too early, so he closed his mouth, put his left hand under the elbow of his right hand, and raised his right hand like a flagpole.

Ms Guan talked for a while more, pointing to Liu Guangting only after she had paused. Liu Guangting stood up and said, 'Teacher, Chen Yanping's home is just across from the school, and he never passes by a snack stand on his way to school!'

Everyone understood what he meant; and Ms Guan understood even more. What he meant was that Chen Yanping was not worthy of praise. Ms Guan said, 'You can't emphasise the objective reasons; it's a person's character and habits—'

"No matter how far his home is from the school, he won't eat snacks because he has no money," interjected Pu Yunsheng.

The classroom suddenly went quiet. Ms Guan stared at Pu Yunsheng, as if seeing him for the first time. He felt slightly embarrassed. 'I'm telling the truth!'

At that moment, someone knocked on the door of the classroom. When it was opened, the children saw Uncle Wang and Uncle Chang from the reception standing at the door. Uncle Wang was holding an enamel washbasin filled with yellow and rosy apricots. Uncle Chang was carrying a sack.

The students chirped curiously.

Uncle Wang said, 'Ms Guan, the school sent us to bring apricots to the students!'

Ms Guan asked, 'Did the other classes receive them, too?'

'Yes, each class received half a washbasin.'

Ms Guan took the apricots and poured them into the white washbasin that was used in the classroom for cleaning. She turned around and asked the students, 'Do you know the big apricot tree in front of the moon gate?'

Everyone said together, 'Yes!'

'These apricots have been picked from that tree. It is huge, and the apricots it bears are very delicious. It's all thanks to everyone's love... No one picked a single apricot. I heard from Principal Xue that the apricots that fell on the ground were picked up by passing students and handed over to the Young Pioneers brigade. Principal Xue said that our apricot tree would make a great story.'

Next, Ms Guan asked the squadron leader, Hu Xingmin, to distribute apricots to everyone. The classroom suddenly erupted. The students stretched their necks like greedy little cats, laughing and shouting.

Ms Guan looked at the apricots in the washbasin, estimated how many there were, and said, 'Let's divide them, and each student can have two. They should be evenly sized.'

After the apricots had been shared out, there were still five left. Ms Guan asked, 'Who hasn't got theirs yet?'

Song Xiaohui said, 'Ms Guan has not got hers yet!'

The students shouted together, 'Ms Guan has not got hers yet!' Ms Guan took two with a smile. Then some of the students shouted, 'Give the rest to Ms Guan!'

'Adults eat a lot!' Liu Guangting said.

Everyone laughed. Ms Guan shook her head.

'Give it to Chen Yanping! He usually doesn't eat snacks,' said Liu Guangting.

'Yes! Give it to him. Their family is the poorest!' Pu Yunsheng also shouted.

'Agreed!' the whole class said together.

Ms Guan Qi and Hu Xingmin walked up to Chen Yanping with the washbasin in their hands, 'Chen Yanping, the students all told me to give you the rest. Please take them.'

Chen Yanping stared, wide-eyed, and shook his head.

‘Take it. You’re welcome!’ Liu Guangting added.

Once again, Chen Yanping shook his head.

Ms Guan Qi asked with concern, ‘What’s the matter? Chen Yanping, everyone has good intentions!’

Chen Yanping’s face went a little red. He stood up and said, ‘Ms Guan, thank you for all your kindness. My mother told me that no matter how poor a person is, he must have dignity!’

There was silence in the classroom for a while, and then the students began to talk in hushed tones. Everyone seemed to understand what Chen Yanping was thinking. He must have been angry with Liu Guangting and Pu Yunsheng.

Ms Guan’s expression became uncertain. She didn’t say anything. She was unsure whether to tell him again to take them or leave him be.

After being silent for a while, Ms Guan touched the top of Chen Yanping’s head again. Little Auspicious suddenly felt that it was right for Teacher Guan to stroke Chen Yanping’s head. If Little Auspicious were a teacher, he would have done the same. It was an expression of comfort and praise.

A few nights later, before Little Auspicious fell asleep, he vaguely heard his mother say to his father, ‘I heard that Chen Yanping lost his father. It was just after the liberation...’

Little Auspicious didn’t hear any other details, but he had heard that one sentence. Chen Yanping didn’t have a father, and something bad had happened. He felt very sorry for Chen Yanping. Did Ms Guan know about Chen Yanping’s father? Did Chen Yanping know? Little Auspicious didn’t want to get up and ask. He knew that adults didn’t want children to know about such things.

With this secret in mind, from then on, whenever Little Auspicious saw Chen Yanping, he always felt a little flustered. Every time he saw Chen Yanping working hard, Little Auspicious always felt that he saw Yanping's mother sitting beside him, mending clothes.

One day, as they were playing together during recess, Pu Yunsheng said, 'Chen Yanping, where is your father?'

Chen Yanping's face became flushed as if he had tuberculosis. After a long pause, he finally answered, 'He is working in another place.'

'Why doesn't he come back?'

Little Auspicious walked up to Pu Yunsheng and said loudly, 'His father has gone to Shanghai.'

'How do you know?'

'I just know his dad works in Shanghai!' Little Auspicious almost shouted.

A few days later, Little Auspicious ate a bowl of braised noodles with shredded pork at Chen Yanping's house. Chen Yanping's mother kept persuading Little Auspicious to eat more, but he saw that the stew left in the pot was not enough for one person, and he knew she hadn't eaten yet.

Little Auspicious never connected the bowl of noodles with what he had said during that recess. Because he had come to Chen Yanping's house by chance that day, Chen Yanping's mother had asked him to stay for dinner.

After returning home, Little Auspicious told his mother about it. Mother said, 'Invite Chen Yanping come to our house to play someday.'

CHAPTER FIFTEEN

Growing Pains

As children grow up, there are more opportunities for them to make mistakes.

One such mistake happened with Liu Guangting.

Liu Guangting and Little Auspicious moved from kindergarten to Number Two Primary School together. They were very good friends.

One day, Liu Guangting brought to school a leather ball with patterns engraved on it. It looked like a softball, but it wasn't one. It was hard and heavy in his hand.

After class, Little Auspicious and Liu Guangting threw the ball to each other. Without thinking, Little Auspicious threw the ball at one of the big windows, and the glass cracked and smashed to the ground. Little Auspicious's first reaction was to pick up the largest piece of glass that had fallen on the ground and try to fix the window by putting it back, but, of course, it was futile.

Several classmates clapped their hands loudly and shouted, 'Ah! You are in trouble!'

Little Auspicious was stunned, and Liu Guangting shared his reaction.

Ms Guan brought Little Auspicious and Liu Guangting back to her office.

'Who broke the window?' She asked.

'He did.' Liu Guangting pointed at Little Auspicious.

'Who brought the ball?'

'He did.' Little Auspicious pointed at Liu Guangting. At that moment, he felt a glimmer of hope. If Liu Guangting hadn't brought that ball to school, Little Auspicious wouldn't have caused such a catastrophe. He felt that Liu Guangting should pay for the broken window.

Little Auspicious's mother was asked to come to the school. It was decided that, of the three yuan that it would cost to replace the glass, Little Auspicious's parents had to pay two and a half yuan and Liu Guangting's parents half a yuan. His mother didn't say anything on the way home. Upon arriving home, she let out a long sigh. Little Auspicious felt discomfort in his heart as if he had been poked by a needle. Two and a half yuan was almost a week's food money for Little Auspicious's family.

Little Auspicious felt that this was the biggest disaster he had ever caused in his life.

Ever since he broke the glass, Little Auspicious felt that he had slipped from the ranks of good students. He started making mistakes, one after another.

Little Auspicious's family lived at No. 9 Dacheng Alley. Sometimes the boys would go to the courtyard of No. 10 to play. At No. 10 lived a girl named Xiaohui who was one year younger than Little Auspicious. One day, Little Auspicious, Xiaohui and Lao Dezi were playing with picture cards on the steps to the door. The cards were half the size of playing cards and had the images of foreign paintings on them. When a picture was facing upwards, a player would slap the step next to the card without touching it. If the picture were turned over by the rush of air created by the player's hand, it was considered a point.

As they were playing, Lao Dezi noticed a two-cent note on the steps, so he shouted, 'Whose money?'

A green two-cent note lay folded in half on the steps, showing part of the image of an aeroplane parked at an airport. Little Auspicious said, 'The money is mine!'

If there was no dispute, Little Auspicious was going to put the banknote in his pocket. But then Xiaohui suddenly touched her pocket and said that the money belonged to her. Her father had given her five cents that morning, and she had bought a sesame seed cake for three cents. And her two cents were missing.

Hearing what Xiaohui said so clearly, Little Auspicious was momentarily at a loss for words. The money might not have been his, but it was not necessarily Xiaohui's, either. So he bit the bullet and started arguing with Xiaohui.

Xiaohui cried.

Xiaohui's father came out of the house. He told Little Auspicious that he had given Xiaohui the money. The verdict was final. Little Auspicious, his face flushing red, took the money out of his pocket and handed it to Xiaohui. Xiaohui's father led her back to the courtyard and closed the door. Lao Dezi had already left. Little Auspicious remained alone on the steps. His stance remained the same – one foot on a step and the other on the ground. Shame welled up in Little Auspicious's heart.

A few days earlier, Little Auspicious had taken a two-cent bill to the small grocery store at the entrance of the alley to buy vinegar. As he came to the shop, he had a feeling that the shopkeeper would give him too much change by mistake.

When people live in poverty, many fantasies arise in their minds. For example, finding money on the ground or, when buying things, receiving extra change. For this sort of fantasy, people will view a one-in-ten-thousand or one-in-a-million possibility as a reality and will think it will come true.

Perhaps it was God's hint that day or the shopkeeper was confused. Little Auspicious's fantasy became a reality. He bought vinegar for two cents and received ninety-eight cents in change. He was very happy, not because he could take advantage of the shopkeeper but because his premonition had come true.

He calmly put the money on the counter and said, 'Shopkeeper, you have given me the wrong change.' The shopkeeper was stunned for a moment. Little Auspicious then said, 'The money I gave you just now was two cents.'

The shopkeeper let out an 'Oh!' and hurriedly took the money back without even a thank you. Little Auspicious was still very happy. Apart from the fulfilment of his premonition, he also felt that he was very honourable.

But what had happened at Xiaohui's place? Why had he been so greedy and shameful? Little Auspicious walked home in a daze. He was afraid that Xiaohui's father would tell his family about what had happened that day, but luckily he didn't. After about a week, Little Auspicious's fear subsided.

When Little Auspicious began attending school, his father kept a record of his daily performance on a paper form, one sheet per month. Every night, his father would fill in the day's performance grade with a pen. The best grade was 'A', general performance was 'B', and the worst performance was 'C'. For many days, Little Auspicious's performance was 'A'.

He began to realise that his performance was not as good as before. Now, if his father asked him about his performance, he would definitely say that he was a 'B+' or even a 'B'.

The alley was empty. Only the wooden telephone poles stretched from the front to the entrance of the alley. One, two, three, four, five – a total of five.

CHAPTER SIXTEEN

Less Than Nine Years Old

The second session in the afternoon was Ms Liu's science class. After the class, she assigned some extracurricular homework. She held a piece of mica ore in her hand, carefully picked it twice with a sewing needle, and a thin amber mica sheet was peeled off, crystal clear, about half the size of a child's palm.

Ms Liu held up the mica sheet, took a piece of horse dung paper and said, 'Everyone please carve a round hole the size of a spectacle lens in the middle of the horse dung paper with a knife. We need to carve two pieces. Then sandwich this piece of mica between the two pieces.' The middle of the horse dung paper was glued with glue, and it was made into a pair of glasses that could be used to watch a solar eclipse. 'There will be a partial solar eclipse in two days, and we can use these glasses to observe it.'

Ms Guan, the head teacher, appeared outside the classroom window. Little Auspicious knew that class would be over soon and that Ms Guan must have something to say to the students.

Ms Liu continued. 'Each of you come and get a small piece of horse manure paper and two pieces of mica. Today's homework is to make a pair of glasses for observing the solar eclipse.'

Cheers of joy rang out together with the bell for the end of class, and the students stood up and bowed to Ms Liu. Ms Guan opened the door and walked into the classroom. The students sat down in their seats and looked up at Ms Guan. Ms Guan had absolute authority in the hearts of the students; no matter how naughty the students were, they dared not bother her. She said, 'After this, the students who have reached the age of nine will stay. The other students can leave.'

Little Auspicious was now in the second grade of primary school. He had started school at the age of six and was now eight years old. Some students had started at seven and were now nine years old.

Why did the classmates who weren't nine years old have to leave? Oh! Little Auspicious suddenly understood that nine was the age for joining the Young Pioneers! The children who stayed would join the league and wear a red scarf.

The students went to the podium to receive mica sheets and horse manure paper. Not many of the children talked about wearing a red scarf. Little Auspicious felt a little strange. He took the horse manure paper and mica sheet, put them between the pages of his book, then returned to his seat and sat down. He looked around nonchalantly and saw that half of his classmates had left the classroom. But he didn't leave. He wanted to wear the red scarf.

Ms Liu nodded to Ms Guan and left. The classroom became quiet. Little Auspicious suddenly felt a little nervous.

Ms Guan watched the students for a while, and when her eyes settled on Little Auspicious, he couldn't help but lower his head slightly.

Ms Guan spoke about joining the Young Pioneers, talking first about the glory of the Young Pioneers. Then she told them that every student who wanted to join needed to fill out an application form. After five minutes, Ms Guan dismissed the class and told them they could go home.

When Little Auspicious was about to go, he was stopped by Ms Guan. She told him to go back to his seat. Then she pulled out the chair in front of him and sat down, facing him as if getting ready for a long chat. His heart pounded.

'Are you now nine years old?'

'Not yet.' Little Auspicious didn't dare lie. Before he finished speaking, he felt that he had done something very wrong – as if he had stolen something. Unexpectedly, he began crying silently, shaking his head while crying.

'Young Pioneers have a rule that you can only join at the age of nine. You can go home now.' Ms Guan patted his head then stood up and left.

At that time, whether you were a Young Pioneer or not, whether you wore a red scarf or not was the difference between being a good student and an ordinary student. Wearing a red scarf meant you were a good student. If you wore the armband of a captain, squadron leader, or even a big squad leader, then you were an excellent student. Joining the Young Pioneers would come sooner or later. Although it was a minimum requirement, not everyone could join the Young Pioneers at the age of nine. It was glorious to join early! Some children did not join the league until they were in the sixth grade of primary school, but where was the glory in that? Joining when older was just a form of comfort for underachievers!

About a week later, the whole school held a meeting of the Young Pioneers. The Young Pioneers lined up in the playground. They wore bright red scarves, white jackets and blue trousers. They looked brilliant! In front of them was the school's drum team. The drum team was majestic, each member wearing a red scarf, and the conductor at the front wore white gloves.

Students who did not wear red scarves also stood in the playground in their different classes. The counsellor, Ms Li, herself wearing a red scarf, announced loudly, 'The Enrolment Ceremony of the Young Pioneers of the Second Affiliated Primary School of Beijing Normal University is now starting! Bring out the flag!'

Accompanied by the drumming sound of 'Dong Dong Qiang Qiang', Song Guiying, a sixth-grade girl wearing the captain's armband, walked past the Young Pioneers holding the brigade flag, which had on it the image of a star torch. She was followed by two flag guards whose arms were raised above their heads. Little Auspicious was very envious. He wondered when he could become a flag bearer.

After the flag-raising ceremony, all the Young Pioneers sang the league's song, 'We, the children of New China; we, the pioneers of new youth…'

In Class One of the second grade that Little Auspicious was in, more than a dozen students had become new members of the Young Pioneers, and they were all wearing white jackets and blue pants and standing at the front of the class.

Red scarves were given to the new team members. Ms Li's face flushed with excitement.

The drums sounded again, and the blaring of the trumpet was extraordinary. The new Young Pioneers walked to the middle of the playground. Most of them were from the second grade. Little Auspicious saw that their faces were full of joy.

The whole ceremony took about half an hour. When the new team members saluted, the counsellor said loudly, 'Students, do you know what it means to put the five fingers of our right hand together and hold them high above our heads? It means that the interests of the people are above all else!'

Little Auspicious secretly made up his mind that in another year, when he was nine years old, he would also raise his right hand high above his head. He looked forward to that day.

CHAPTER SEVENTEEN

Hold Mother's Hand

Every year on the National Day, the First of October, Tiananmen Square in Beijing would hold celebrations. In the morning, there was a military parade and a mass civilian parade, and in the evening, there was a fireworks show. Everyone danced together to the music in the square.

Because of their age, pupils below fifth grade were given a holiday on that day, and students who had no assignments did not have to go to school. At that time, television sets were very rare, and ordinary people could not watch TV. Without a television, many people gathered around a 'chatterbox' (radio) to listen to the broadcast. The broadcast mainly featured the famous announcers Qi Yue, Xia Qing and Ge Lan describing the events at Tiananmen Square as they happened. Their voices seemed give their audience a pair of eyes and lead everyone to Tiananmen Square.

Little Auspicious also listened to the radio, but on several National Days, his mother took him to Chang'an Avenue to watch the parade. Chang'an Avenue is where Little Auspicious saw tanks and armoured vehicles and planes flying in formation for the first time in his life.

On festival days, the streets on both sides of Chang'an Avenue were controlled by soldiers, and tram and car traffic were halted. Little Auspicious needed to walk to the Xidan intersection of Chang'an Avenue. It was about ten tram stops from his home in Dacheng Alley to the Xidan intersection.

Why go to the Xidan intersection? Because there he could see the parade coming from Tiananmen Square.

The celebration usually started at ten o'clock in the morning and was announced by the mayor of Beijing. After the commander's inspection was completed, the troops would first march through Tiananmen slowly, and planes would fly across the sky. After the troops had passed out of Tiananmen Square, their speed would increase, and they would pass through Xidan a quarter of an hour later for the crowds of people 'watching the excitement' to feast their eyes. Thus, Little Auspicious and his mother aimed to arrive at Xidan just after ten o'clock.

The section of Chang'an Avenue from Xidan to Dongdan was controlled by soldiers. Except for parade participants, ordinary pedestrians were not allowed through. The parade marched west from Tiananmen Square, and when they arrived in Xidan, they thrilled the crowd with their perfect formation. When the tanks and armoured vehicles passed by, everyone was still very excited. Many ordinary people watched the excitement alongside Little Auspicious at the Xidan intersection.

In addition to the troops, a mass civilian parade passed through Tiananmen Square in square formations, composed roughly of honour guards, Young Pioneers, workers' teams, farmers' teams, student teams, government officials, ethnic minorities, militias, literary and art troops, and sports troops. There were also float drivers and people who carried the portraits of leaders, large slogans, flags, bouquets, doves of peace and balloons.

中華人民共和國萬歲
人民大團結萬

Unfortunately, the beautiful balloons and doves of peace were released in Tiananmen Square. Many of the parade teams dispersed before reaching Xidan; some turned into Nanchang Street, and some turned into Liubukou, to the disappointment of the patient crowd of common people.

The tanks and cannons excited everyone, and so did the army of sports and literature and art. Actors of the Literary Army stood on the floats in costumes and posed as characters. Male and female athletes on the float surrounded by the sports army were wearing swimsuits, even though it was cold in Beijing in October and everyone else wore sweaters. When they saw the athletes in swimsuits looking stiff from the cold, people jokingly called them the salted duck team. Little Auspicious shivered for them.

When the teams arrived in Xidan, some of them acted as if they had completed their parade. They didn't do anything but walk in lines. Other teams were still in good formation. Under the leadership of their conductors, they continued to perform, to the gratitude of the spectators.

After watching the parade, Little Auspicious was really tired on the way home. He and his mother had to sit on the kerb to rest for a while at almost every tram stop. It was very tiring for his mother to pull Little Auspicious up onto his feet every time they started walking again.

Another year, when they were going home from the parade, they heard a 'dang! dang! dang!' sound coming up from the behind. It was a tram coming to a stop next to them. Little Auspicious's mother took him home on the tram. The tickets cost five cents each. For some reason, that day, Little Auspicious insisted on holding his own ticket. He saw many adults sticking tickets to their lips after receiving them, and he thought it looked like fun. He knelt on the bench by the window and stuck the ticket to his lips. His mother told him it was unhygienic. Little Auspicious took the ticket off his lips and accidentally dropped it between the seat and the window. When they were getting off the tram, the conductor saw that Little Auspicious had no ticket, and he insisted that Little Auspicious's mother buy another one. His mother tried to explain what had happened, but it was to no avail. She had to spend another five cents.

After getting out of the tram, his mother walked off without even looking at Little Auspicious. She was angry. He didn't dare fall behind, so he ran to catch up with her. At that moment, he especially hoped that his mother would turn around and hold his hand.

His mother continued to ignore him, and Little Auspicious felt like bursting into tears.

Just then, his mother abruptly turned around and looked at Little Auspicious. 'You need to be more careful in the future, okay?'

His mother stretched out her hand, and Little Auspicious ran over to her happily. He would never forget the warmth of that moment.

CHAPTER EIGHTEEN

Honour

A year passed, and Little Auspicious was now old enough to join the Young Pioneers. However, the conditions for joining the brigade were becoming more and more stringent. Not only did students have to be old enough, but they also needed outstanding performances in the moral, intellectual and physical aspects of their education. So Little Auspicious worked harder.

One day, Ms Guan announced that ten outstanding students and fifteen advanced students would be selected from the class. She showed the certificates to everyone: pink for outstanding students and sky blue for advanced students. Little Auspicious looked longingly at the certificates. He really wanted a pink certificate, but he suddenly felt that he wasn't outstanding. He would be happy to get a certificate for being an advanced student.

The selection process for awarding the certificates was very democratic. First, the students had to be nominated by their classmates. The teacher would write the names of the nominated students on the blackboard, and then everyone would vote. Finally, based on the number of votes, the teacher would determine which of them were excellent students and which were advanced students.

The teacher said, 'Let's think about it first and make some preparations today. We will formally nominate and vote in the afternoon class assembly.' Then she spread the student's report cards on the table again and read them solemnly.

During the class break, Little Auspicious heard someone calling his name. When he looked around, he saw his good friends Yang Yinpu and Liu Guangting.

Yang Yinpu leaned over and asked in a low voice, 'Do you want to be an advanced student?'

'Who would vote for us? Someone must vote!' Little Auspicious said.

'Little Auspicious votes for Liu Guangting, Liu Guangting votes for me, and I vote for Little Auspicious. Let's create a voting circle.'

'Okay,' Little Auspicious replied, with some reluctance, after hesitating for a moment.

'Keep it a secret! This way, we will all be advanced students!' Liu Guangting said this to comfort his guilty conscience.

'Okay! If anyone tells, he isn't human!' Yang Yinpu said.

During the afternoon class assembly, the selection of the outstanding students began. As expected, Little Auspicious's name did not appear on the blackboard. Ms Guan stood in front of the blackboard with chalk and, from time to time, cast encouraging glances at the students who were about to raise their hands for nominations.

Finally, the selection of the advanced students began. This time, the students made nominations enthusiastically, and everyone felt that that they had a chance of being an advanced student.

One by one, the names of the children elected to be advanced students appeared on the blackboard. Little Auspicious counted them silently.

Little Auspicious couldn't sit still anymore. Yang Yinpu and Liu Guangting looked at Little Auspicious from time to time. Little Auspicious finally stood up bravely, tried his best to avoid Teacher Guan's gaze, and said with almost closed eyes, 'I choose Liu Guangting!' After speaking, he quickly sat down.

Ms Guan nodded, and Liu Guangting's name was written on the blackboard. Liu Guangting's eyes lit up.

About five minutes later, the names of Little Auspicious and Yang Yinpu were also written on the blackboard.

Finally, all the students in the class raised their hands and made their selections, and all three of the boys had been nominated to become advanced students.

Ms Guan looked over the whole class with calm, majestic eyes. When she looked at Little Auspicious, he saw something strange in her gaze. Subconsciously, he looked away from Ms Guan, but when he closed his eyes, he still felt Ms Guan's gaze on his face. Under the effect of that gaze, Little Auspicious felt as if he had become a transparent body. His heart was beating wildly.

'I'll check the grades of the selected students again, and I will issue a certificate tomorrow!' Ms Guan said.

After class, Yang Yinpu and Liu Guangting rushed out the door like rabbits. But when Little Auspicious was about to leave the classroom, Ms Wang stopped him, 'Little Auspicious, come to the office.'

'Tell me, why did you choose Liu Guangting?' she asked casually while correcting homework.

'He has improved...and he works hard,' Little Auspicious said.

'Yesterday, the whole class wiped the windows, but he ran away!' The teacher looked up from the homework and stared at Little Auspicious.

'I don't know.' Little Auspicious lowered his eyes.

'Look up. Think about what you want to say to your teacher.' Although Miss Guan asked this casually, Little Auspicious felt it was time to decide, he needed to either tell the truth or deny it. If Yang Yinpu and Liu Guangting were present, Little Auspicious might have told the truth. But they weren't there, and he couldn't break the promise he'd made with them behind their backs.

Little Auspicious was in great pain now. Looking up, he saw Ms Guan's grey hair. No one knew how much of her hair had turned grey because of the students. Voting for each other was a bit villain-like. He could no longer lie, and he felt sorry for lying to Ms Guan.

But what about Yang Yinpu and Liu Guangting? If they didn't mention it to other people, how could he?

'Did Liu Guangting ask you to choose him?' Ms Guan asked suddenly.

No, I did it voluntarily,' Little Auspicious whispered.

During class the next day, Ms Guan walked into the classroom with a stack of awards. The students immediately became attentive. Both Yang Yinpu and Liu Guangting looked at the ceiling. Little Auspicious was also a little nervous.

'The most precious thing for a person is honesty,' Ms Guan stated. 'However, in our election yesterday, three students were dishonest. In order to get the certificate, they voted for one another. But two students were able to recognise their mistakes and tell their teacher the truth.'

Little Auspicious was stunned.

'I have approved the qualifications of those two students as advanced students, but the other student cannot be rewarded until he realises his mistake.'

The classroom suddenly fell silent. Everyone looked at each other with inquiring eyes.

Little Auspicious's heart sank.

The teacher began to announce the list of advanced students. That was the most painful time for Little Auspicious. Yang Yinpu and Liu Guangting were on the list, but he was not. Little Auspicious discovered that he was the least advanced in his class!

After school, there was joy in the classroom, and many students went home with their awards to announce the good news to their parents. Little Auspicious hoped that his two friends could come to him and comfort him. But the classroom was almost empty, and they didn't come. Little Auspicious had no choice but to blame himself. He had really wanted to scold them, but he hadn't. Weren't they justified?

Little Auspicious wanted to cry, but what was the point? Yang Yinpu had come up with this idea the day before, and then he told the teacher that he had done something wrong! Despite thinking of the reason for his grievance, Little Auspicious still couldn't cry.

It was not over. A new batch of Young Pioneers would be approved, and in a few days, the list would be posted on the bulletin board at the school gate.

When school ended that afternoon and Little Auspicious was walking to the school gate, the counsellor, Ms Li, called him to the brigade headquarters. Teacher Li said to him, 'The list of new players will be announced soon. This time, your name is missing, showing you still have shortcomings. Don't be discouraged. Work hard and strive for the next batch so that you can join the Young Pioneers.'

Little Auspicious couldn't help but shed tears as he walked out of the school. The way home seemed so long that day.

Two days later, the doorbell rang just after dinner. It was Uncle Qu from Xiaocheng Alley, accompanied by Yang Yinpu.

Yang Yinpu greeted Little Auspicious when he saw him. Little Auspicious found it very strange.

Uncle Qu was a well-known martial arts practitioner in the area. Everyone knew him. He had three long beards on his chin. Little Auspicious's parents politely invited Uncle Qu in to sit down. Uncle Qu pointed to Yang Yinpu and said, 'This is my grandson. I have come here today specially to apologise to Little Auspicious.'

Little Auspicious's parents were shocked, and Little Auspicious was also surprised.

When Yang Yinpu had returned home the day before yesterday, he had shown the advanced student certificate to his parents and Uncle Qu. The family praised Yang Yinpu's progress. Yang Yinpu was a little prideful, so he talked about Little Auspicious's advanced student certificate being retracted. Uncle Qu listened carefully. The more he listened, the more interested he became. After hearing Yang Yinpu speak, his brows furrowed tightly.

He asked him, 'Did you come up with this idea?'

'Yes, it was me.'

'Did you admit it when the teacher asked?'

Yang Yinpu nodded.

'Did Little Auspicious admit it?'

'He is more stubborn, and he still doesn't admit it. The teacher is angry.'

Uncle Qu asked Yang Yinpu to stand before him and said with a stern face, 'You've tricked him, don't you know?'

Yang Yinpu became nervous.

Little Auspicious's parents didn't know what had happened at school. They had only seen that Little Auspicious had had something on his mind recently. Having heard what Uncle Qu said, they now understood the whole story.

Uncle Qu said to Little Auspicious, 'You made a mistake. The election should not be tampered with; it should be aboveboard!'

Little Auspicious nodded.

Uncle Qu pointed at Yang Yinpu again, raised his voice, and said, 'But *you* made two mistakes. First, you made a "circle selection", which was the first mistake. Then you told the teacher Little Auspicious was involved. When you said this, did you think that it would hurt other people? You acted disloyally to your friends, and this was your second mistake!'

Everyone was stunned. No one had expected that Uncle Qu would scold his grandson like that in front of strangers. Little Auspicious felt something warm rushing from his heart to his throat. He really wanted to cry, but he held back.

Uncle Qu said to Little Auspicious's father, 'I asked him to apologise to your child today.'

But his father quickly said, 'Why, Uncle Qu? The bumps between children are part of growing up. You take it too seriously. We really shouldn't take it so seriously! Little Auspicious, hurry up and thank Uncle Qu!'

Little Auspicious did not speak. Yang Yinpu took out his certificate and handed it to Little Auspicious. 'Here, this is for you.'

Little Auspicious's father laughed. 'Look, this is how children are!'

'I can't join the Young Pioneers anymore!' Little Auspicious cried out.

Everyone was stunned. Little Auspicious's tears, which he had been holding back for a long time, now flowed down his face. Uncle Qu's words had been like a small hand stroking his heart. He couldn't take it any longer.

Uncle Qu asked about the situation, squinted his eyes and thought for a while. Then, without saying anything, he patted the top of Little Auspicious's head, stood up and took Yang Yinpu away.

The school once again held a grand inauguration for new brigade members. Yang Yinpu, Liu Guangting and the other new members all wore white jackets and blue trousers. They lined up in front of the small podium.

Little Auspicious sat on the side with the other students who had not yet joined the brigade. He felt alone; there were not many students in his class who had not joined the Young Pioneers.

This time, the team leader hosted the meeting. She began to announce the list of new students joining the Young Pioneers. The list of new members included Little Auspicious's name! He was stunned! Had the leader read it wrong? He couldn't believe his ears.

Ms Guan came over hurriedly, 'Little Auspicious, hurry up!'

He didn't know how he had been accepted into the brigade. He felt his face getting hot. There were countless pairs of eyes looking at him.

The senior Young Pioneers helped the new members put on their red scarves, and the drum team began to play. Both Liu Guangting and Yang Yinpu wore red scarves. Little Auspicious also put on his red scarf and stood alongside them.

Ms Li the counsellor asked, 'Students, do you know what it means to put the five fingers of our right hand together and hold them high above our heads? That means that the interests of the people are above all else!'

The new team members replied in unison, 'The interests of the people are above all else!'

When Little Auspicious raised his right hand above his head, his left hand stroked the red scarf, and he couldn't help thinking of Uncle Qu. He would always remember Uncle Qu's visit, his long beard fluttering in the wind.

CHAPTER NINETEEN

Uncle Zhao From the Little South House

The house in Little Auspicious's courtyard was divided into four parts: the north house in the front yard, the north house in the back yard, the west house in the back yard, and the lonely south house near the door. The houses in the front yard had wooden flooring set half a metre above the ground, and when people stepped hard on the floorboards, there would be a 'dong, dong' sound. Unlike the houses in the front yard, the backyard was paved with tiles, and it would always be neat and beautiful after being cleaned with a mop. Only the floor of the south house was paved with grey bricks – the lowest standard. When the yard was built, the south room functioned as the reception room for the whole yard. There was a telephone in the reception room, which was very rare at the time. No one knew why, but the family members called the south house the Little South House.

Little Auspicious's family had once been rich, but not overly so. His father used to own a bank, and Big Auspicious had enjoyed its benefits. But not Little Auspicious, who had been born later. Their father had often taken Big Auspicious to eat somewhere called 'on the counter' where there were also at least two round tables with people eating at them. Their father's bank was a small business, but even this small business had been the target of a scam. A tax official had deposited two pieces of gold in the bank. Little Auspicious's father had returned it to him before liberation but had forgotten to ask him for the IOU. After the liberation, the official was arrested, and his wife came to the bank with the IOU demanding to be paid back the gold. Little Auspicious's father was stunned. He was loyal to others, and he wanted to save face. He had never expected that someone would treat him so poorly, so he gritted his teeth and said that he would pay back her money even if he had to sell everything. It was easy to say, but he had to close down the bank. Where would he get the money to pay back the two pieces of gold? This may have been the reason why Little Auspicious seldom saw his father smile. Later, the 'official' was released. He had no idea what his wife had done, but it was too late. He didn't even have a job to earn a living, and his wife had run away with someone else.

Little Auspicious's mother said that his father was not a businessman, and his father himself said that he would not do business if there were another way to earn a living.

Although Little Auspicious's family lived in the north house, which was the best, the family was busy making a living every day. There no longer was a reception room, and the telephone had been removed. At the very beginning, Little South House was the family's guest room. Little Auspicious's father's friends and relatives from his hometown stayed in it when they came to Beijing.

When Little Auspicious was in second grade, Uncle Zhao lived in the Little South House. Uncle Zhao was very lonely, so whenever he was free, he asked Little Auspicious to come over and chat.

After they started growing vegetables at home, Little Auspicious's chores became harder. Little Auspicious previously had only to water two grapevines, but now he watered vegetables daily. His first task after school every day was to water them. The faucet was next to the peony pond in the front yard. He used an iron bucket to carry the water to the back yard.

One day, while he was watering the vegetables, Uncle Zhao called him over.

When Little Auspicious came in, Uncle Zhao pointed to a chair. 'Come, sit down.'

He sat down obediently, realising that Uncle Zhao was going to tell him something important. Uncle Zhao was a friend of his father's and was older than him. In Little Auspicious's mind, Uncle Zhao was already an old man, but in fact, he was only in his fifties. He did not know if he had a home or why he lived in the Little South House. Little Auspicious knew only that Uncle Zhao often cooked on the stove alone and that the food was not entirely clean.

'Come, write a letter for me!'

'I don't know how to write a letter,' Little Auspicious said honestly.

'It's okay. I say, you write.'

'What kind of pen do you use?'

'Just use your pen. What kind of pen do you have?'

I only have a pencil and a ballpoint pen, but my dad won't let me use the ballpoint pen. He said if I used it now, I wouldn't be able to write well in the future.'

'It doesn't matter; you don't use it often. Just use a ballpoint pen!'

Little Auspicious ran back to his room and took the ballpoint pen. When he returned, Uncle Zhao had already spread the letter paper on the table. 'You write: *Pheasant Wei Yunpu, I think back to when...*'

Little Auspicious turned to look at Uncle Zhao. He didn't understand what Uncle Zhao meant. In the past, when he had watched his father writing letters, he saw that he would always start with 'Your honourable Sir' or something similar. 'Pheasant' was a curse word. The word 'rogue' was used when insulting a man and 'pheasant' when insulting a woman. Besides, adults didn't allow children to say these two words. If children said the words aloud, the adults would say coldly, 'Do you want to be beaten?'

'Write!' Uncle Zhao rapped the table with his knuckles, his face full of anger. Little Auspicious did not know if Uncle Zhao was angry with him or the woman.

> Pheasant Wei Yunpu, I think back to when the big-headed me, Zhao Heting, took you and your daughter in when you were in distress, provided you with food, drink, and clothing. But now, unexpectedly, you are so ungrateful...

The letter was not long. After writing it, Little Auspicious had a general idea of the situation. Wei Yunpu was an ungrateful woman whom Uncle Zhao had helped. The main content of the letter was him cursing her.

After Little Auspicious had finished writing the letter, Uncle Zhao rummaged through an old paper bag and took out a piece of peach cake. He passed it to Little Auspicious, but he waved his hand to decline it. First, his father forbade him from taking things from other people, and second, he thought that Uncle Zhao's things were always dirty. By now, Uncle Zhao had returned to his former amiable appearance. Little Auspicious felt that Uncle Zhao was very pitiful and that the woman must be a bad person.

When Little Auspicious came out from Little South House, his mother asked him what he had been doing in Uncle Zhao's house. Little Auspicious said he had written a letter for Uncle Zhao and told her of the letter's content. His mother was shocked. Later, she told Little Auspicious's father and asked him, 'How can Uncle Zhao let a child write such things?' His father did not reply.

The next afternoon, Uncle Zhao ran into Little Auspicious beside the rockery and asked him quietly, 'Little Auspicious, did you tell your mother about the letter?'

Little Auspicious nodded.

Uncle Zhao sighed sadly and went back to the Little South House. Little Auspicious watched him as he lifted the curtain and entered, and felt a little sorry for him.

One day after school, Little Auspicious wanted to cheer up Uncle Zhao, so he came to the Little South House to talk to him. He told him, 'I will recite what I've learned a school!'

Uncle Zhao nodded.

Little Auspicious recited the text he had just learned:

> My family has ten chickens, one hen and nine chicks.
> Once I gave them rice to eat.
> The hen came running, and it ate while crowing, 'Clack, clack, cluck! Cluck, cluck,
> heck!' to call the little chicks to eat.
> The little chicks are coming. The little chicks are coming, eating the rice while calling:
> 'Chirp, chirp, chirp, chirp, chirp, chirp!'

A smile returned to Uncle Zhao's face.

Chapter Twenty

A Special Day

One day, Big Auspicious brought home a book titled *Tanya.* It told the story of the struggle between the Soviet heroine Tanya and the German fascist devils. At the end of the story, Tanya is hanged on the gallows by the German devils. A few days later, Little Auspicious's sister brought home another book called *The Story of Zoya and Shura.* Their elder brother said, 'Let me read it first.' But she said, 'You can read it after I've finished reading it.'

Big Auspicious said, 'I heard that the Zoya in your book is actually named Tanya.'

'If you know so much, why must you read it?'

Big Auspicious said, 'Do you know *How the Steel Was Tempered*?'

'Of course!'

'Do you know who the author is?'

'Pavel Korchagin.'

Big Auspicious smiled. 'Ha! That's wrong! Pavel is the main character of the novel. The author is Ostrovsky.'

Little Auspicious's sister stopped talking.

Little Auspicious thought that maybe his brother was right. Otherwise, why hadn't his sister spoken up? But then, unexpectedly, his sister said, 'Can you recite a passage from the book?'

'Which passage?'

In reply, she began reciting:

> The most precious thing for a person is life. Life is only once for everyone. A person's life should be spent like this: when looking back on the past, he will not regret wasting his time, nor will he be ashamed for doing nothing; Before passing away, he can say: 'My whole life and all my energies have been devoted to the most magnificent cause in the world – the struggle for the liberation of human beings.

Both brothers were stunned. They hadn't expected their sister to be able to recite such a long passage. Although Little Auspicious hadn't quite understood it, he had vaguely sensed the power of those words.

Primary school students would often sing a nursery rhyme:

> The big brother of the Soviet Union earns more money, buys a motorcycle, and drives to Moscow. The old lady in the United States earns less money and buys a small watch; how beautiful is that...

In the minds of primary school students, the Soviets were rich, and Americans were poor. The Soviets were generous, and Americans were stingy.

Teachers and parents often said that the Soviet Union was the big brother, and China was the little brother, and that the Soviet Union today was China tomorrow. Almost all Chinese people knew about Stalin. Although most people had not seen him in person, there were pictures of him everywhere, showing him wearing a marshal's uniform, with a short moustache, and looking very dignified. He was a great leader of the Soviet Union and a good friend to the Chinese people.

In March 1953, the weather was still cold and gloomy. Little Auspicious wore a cotton coat.

One morning, Mr Zhao walked into the classroom, put down his book, coughed and then looked at his students. Mr Zhao was usually a very lively teacher, but that day he seemed to be different.

Mr Zhao looked around the classroom, seemingly looking at each student. Then he said sadly, 'Students, let me tell you some sad news. Stalin has passed away.'

Although primary school students all knew about Stalin, they didn't understand how important he was. But the actions and dignified expressions of the adults following the news left a deep impression on Little Auspicious. He knew this was a very serious matter and something that he should be sad about.

On that day, the atmosphere in the school became tense and sombre, and the words of teachers and classmates became sparse. The students received several notices that day. One of the notices said: *From the 7th of March, for three days, flags across the country will be flown at half-mast, and three days of mourning will be held. A nationwide memorial service is to be held on the 9th of March.*

When the students went to school the next day, they all wore black armbands. Because each household had made armbands for their children, there were wide and narrow ones. Back then, armbands were not made of black gauze. Some students had black cloth strips tied around their arms.

On the afternoon of the 9th of March, the whole country held a memorial service, and a grand memorial ceremony was held in Tiananmen Square.

Little Auspicious and his classmates and teachers gathered on the school's playground. In addition to black armbands, everyone wore small white flowers on their chests.

They watched as the flag-raiser raised the national flag halfway and then stopped. At that moment, the sound of alarms seemed to come from everywhere, from far to near and low to high. The sirens of the factories in the city sounded in unison, echoing each other. Little Auspicious heard the sounds of many kinds of sirens – factory sirens, train sirens, city sirens. It felt as if the whole world was mourning. A funeral dirge broadcast on the radio came out over the speakers, and everyone lowered their heads together.

In the classroom before the school mourning ceremony, some of the girls had tied black strings on their pigtails. Yang Yinpu had put his long hair to one side, then he had intertwined it with white paper and tied it into a small braid, which had made him look like a clown. When they were standing in line, the teacher from the teaching office had seen Yang Yinpu. He had been dragged out of the team, made to take off his headband, and then made to stand behind the whole class. Little Auspicious had seen him crying.

When Little Auspicious got home, his brother and sister had also just returned from school. Neither their father nor mother had a work unit nor had they gone to work, and they had been unable to attend the memorial service. They listened to their children talking about what had happened at school that day, and they were very sombre.

The next morning, Little Auspicious left for school with his schoolbag on his back and saw Mr Lao taking pictures in the yard. Back then, ordinary people did not have cameras. If people wanted photos, they had them taken in photo studios. But Mr Lao had a camera. That day, he was taking pictures of a crab apple tree that had just sprouted leaves.

When Little Auspicious passed through the rockery arch, Mr Lao saw him and waved to him. Little Auspicious walked to the crab apple tree. The old gentleman asked him, 'Why are you wearing a black band on your arm?' Little Auspicious replied, 'Everyone who commemorates Stalin must wear a black band to mourn.'

Mr Lao asked Little Auspicious to sit on the high steps in front of the north room.

He pointed to the black band on Little Auspicious's arm and signalled for him to take it off. But Little Auspicious shook his head and said, 'I have to wear it for these days of mourning, and I have to check it when I enter the school. This is what the teacher said. How can I take it off at home?' Mr Lao nodded understandingly and pressed the shutter of the camera.

Two days later, Little Auspicious received the photo. The boy in the photo seemed to be a bit bloated and slightly chubbier than Little Auspicious in reality. He had a smile on his face and a black band on his arm. Little Auspicious kept this photo with him for many years, and it became a memento of that year.

CHAPTER TWENTY-ONE

A Crow Drinks Water

Children in Beijing called crows 'old ravens'. In winter, the branches without leaves stretched out to the sky. If a few old ravens were to fly past cawing, the scene would be even more bleak.

People also regarded the old raven as a bad omen. If they heard an old raven cawing a few times when they went out, it would make them feel downcast.

One day, Ms Guan told the students that they each needed to find two small stones. Not too big – just the size of a finger joint. They needed to bring them to Chinese class on Monday.

Little Auspicious, like his classmates, picked up two small stones in his spare time. When Monday came, nobody knew what to do with the stones they had picked up.

Ms Guan entered the classroom and put a large glass bottle on the podium. The bottle was filled halfway with pale pink water.

The students asked curiously, 'Ms Guan, what is this for?'

Ms Guan smiled but didn't speak. Then she turned around and removed a black origami sculpture from the handout folder. She unfolded the origami for everyone to see. Wow! It was an old raven!

Ms Guan took the old raven to the glass bottle and inserted it into the mouth of the bottle, and the old raven stood firmly on top of the glass bottle. Little Auspicious saw the old raven's mouth protruding a little into the mouth of the bottle but still far above the water.

Ms Guan pointed to the old raven and asked, 'Students, can this crow drink the water in the bottle?'

'No!' answered everyone, in unison.

'Would we like to help it drink the water?'

'Yes!'

'Then, everyone, take out the pebbles you brought!'

Up until now, the students had forgotten about their pebbles. Everyone either reached into their pockets or opened their pencil cases and took out their pebbles.

Teacher Guan asked the students to line up at the podium, starting with the first group nearest the classroom door, to drop their pebbles into the bottle. Ms Guan said, 'Now each of us is a little crow, and we put the stones we brought into the bottle.'

The classroom erupted in excitement, and as the students queued up, many of them imitated the call of the old raven.

The pink water splashed as each student carefully dropped in their pebbles. The pebbles looked colourful and very beautiful at the bottom of the bottle.

'What do you see?' asked Ms Guan.

'The water level has risen.'

When it was Little Auspicious's to drop in his stones, he saw that the water level was already at crow's beak.

'Teacher, the old raven's beak is wet.'

Ms Guan stretched out her hand to temporarily stop the students behind Little Auspicious. 'Students, what do you see?'

'The crow has drunk the water!' the students shouted together.

'Why can the crow drink water?'

'Because the crow will always find a way.'

Ms Guan asked the students to sit down in their seats, then she opened a book. The text for that day was *A Crow Drinks Water*.

That night, Little Auspicious dreamed that the paper crow on the glass bottle drank all the water and then flew up into the classroom.

CHAPTER TWENTY-TWO

The Story of the Coping Saw

Ms Liu the science teacher was transferred away. Her replacement was a young teacher named Ms Zhang. Ms Zhang had just graduated from a normal school, and she was very serious about teaching. After class, she also taught students how to make small wooden benches and how to raise rabbits. Everyone especially liked her class, and no one was afraid of her.

One day in class, Ms Zhang drew an archery bow on the blackboard.

Little Auspicious said to Yang Yinpu beside him, 'It doesn't look like that at all!'

Yang Yinpu said, 'Like a moon.'

Ms Zhang seemed to have heard their conversation. She said, 'Anyone who talks anymore will leave.'

Little Auspicious thought she was bluffing, so he kept talking. 'It looks like a pancake!'

Before he had finished talking, Teacher Zhang pointed to Little Auspicious and said, 'Stand outside the classroom. Go!'

Little Auspicious had never been treated like this before, and he felt a little scared.

Just then, Yang Yinpu blurted out, 'It's not wrong to know a mistake and correct it!'

Ms Zhang was stunned momentarily. Then she said, 'How does he know he was wrong?'

'You could ask him if he knew he was wrong! You haven't asked him yet,' said Yang Yinpu.

Ms Zhang got angry and pointed at Yang Yinpu, '*You* go out, too!' Yang Yinpu didn't seem to be afraid at all. He walked out very calmly.

Standing at the door of the classroom, Little Auspicious was very nervous. How had he changed from being a good student to one who had been kicked out by the teacher?

Outside the classroom, Yang Yinpu asked Little Auspicious, 'Do you want to play table tennis after class?'

Little Auspicious was stunned for a moment. He was very surprised. Why was Yang Yinpu like this? He was not concerned at all that he had been kicked out by the teacher, and he was still thinking about playing table tennis!

'I am the Jiang Yongning of our school,' Yang Yinpu continued. At that time, table tennis was very popular in primary schools. The school had built two wooden table tennis tables for the students and placed them behind the small bushes next to a small podium. As soon as the bell rang for the end of class, the students would rush out of the classroom and stand in line at the podium.

Jiang Yongning was the national men's singles champion. He was the player most admired by the boys, and Sun Meiying, the women's singles champion, was most admired by the girls. Everyone knew that Jiang Yongning and Sun Meiying were also husband and wife.

Little Auspicious wanted to say that the best table tennis player in the class was actually not Yang Yinpu but Huang Qiang, but he couldn't say it.

Ms Zhang called them in.

'Do you know what you did wrong?'

Yang Yinpu said loudly, 'I know!'

Little Auspicious said, softly, 'I know.'

Everyone could see that Yang Yinpu did not mean it.

Little Auspicious looked at the blackboard and saw that Ms Zhang had drawn not a bow but a saw. It was a coping saw.

Ms Zhang handed out a thick piece of bamboo about sixty centimetres long and five centimetres wide to each student. Then she told everyone to use a knife and sandpaper to process the rough bamboo pieces until they were smooth.

Little Auspicious took the bamboo piece home. His brother told him that scraping bamboo with broken glass was much more effective than doing it with a knife. Little Auspicious tried it and found that the broken glass was really sharp. It took about half a day. He scraped with glass and polished with sandpaper.

The bamboo pieces that everyone brought back three days later to the next science class were no longer rough but smooth and pleasing to the eye.

Ms Zhang asked the students to carve their names on the bamboo pieces with a knife. Then she put all the bamboo pieces into a pond.

Two weeks later, she scooped up the bamboo pieces from the water and then bent them with her hands. Surprisingly, each bamboo piece stayed bent, in the shape of a bow. She held up one of them and said, 'This is the bow of a coping saw.'

The students' eyes widened in amazement. The water was so powerful!

Ms Zhang took out a steel wire, both ends of which had loops formed in them. Ms Zhang said that the steel wire could only be bent into such a small loop when the temperature was very high. Ms Zhang had had to go to a factory to get them made.

Then, using a hand drill, she drilled holes into both ends of a bamboo piece. A nail was inserted into each hole, and the pointed ends of the nails were bent into hooks. The 'nail hooks' were fixed to both ends of the bamboo piece.

Ms Zhang took a chisel and said, 'This kind of chisel is harder than steel.' Then, she took a steel strip and punched some small teeth in it using the chisel. While doing it, she said, 'This is the saw blade. You can't make this. You have to punch a small hole in it without cutting it all the way through." Finally, she fixed the ends of the saw blade onto the nail hooks. Because the bamboo slice was elastic, once it was released, the steel blade was pulled tight.

Ms Zhang raised the bow high. 'This is a coping saw.'

The students applauded.

Only then did Little Auspicious fully understand that what Ms Zhang had drawn on the blackboard that day was a coping saw.

Little Auspicious looked at Ms Zhang with admiration in his heart. He had learned so many things. For example, a coping saw could be used to turn a corner when sawing wood. If one wanted to cut a round hole in the middle of a board, one just needed to remove the blade and put it through the drill hole first.

Ms Zhang took a pencil and drew a circle the size of a pot lid on a piece of plywood. Then she cut a perfect circle in the plywood using the saw she had just made.

The students applauded enthusiastically.

She handed out bamboo pieces to everyone and then put the steel wire onto each student's bow. Then she passed out pieces of plywood to everyone, and she told everyone that the homework was for everyone to use their own saw to cut out a bookend to their own pattern based on their zodiac sign – a chicken or a monkey or a dog. Most of Little Auspicious's classmates were born in the Year of the Chicken, several in the Year of the Monkey, and one or two in the Year of the Dog.

On the way home from school that day, each student held their own wire bow saw, and they all looked like archers!

When Little Auspicious got home, he went under the jujube tree, put the plywood on the stool, and began to cut the plywood. He wanted to make his bookends in the shapes of two chickens – a rooster and a hen.

It started very smoothly. When cutting the rooster's outline, he made it all the way to the beak, which was the most difficult part. Unexpectedly, when the saw was halfway through the plywood, the steel wire suddenly broke, and one end of the steel wire went through Little Auspicious's left hand. It went in through his palm and out the back of his hand, sticking out by about an inch. Little Auspicious was stunned. He looked at his hand in surprise. There was no bleeding, and he didn't feel any pain. He didn't feel scared. He carefully pulled the steel wire out of his hand.

Blood began to come out, but not much, and the fingers could still move. It hadn't hit the bone, so Little Auspicious felt at ease. He walked into the house and only then began to call his mother.

His mother brought the red medicine and looked at his hand. Little Auspicious put some of the medicine on himself, and his mother wrapped his hand in gauze.

The next day, Little Auspicious came to school. The students saw that his hand was bandaged and, one after another, they asked him about it. Little Auspicious said proudly, 'The steel wire went in from this side and out from there!'

'Ah! You still came to school!' Everyone exclaimed.

After class, Little Auspicious ran to the table tennis table as usual. When it was his turn, he held up his injured left hand as he played. Because of this, Little Auspicious became a hero to his classmates. Everyone said that the injury did not keep him from the front line and that Little Auspicious was Jiang Yongning for the day!

Little Auspicious had not expected to receive everyone's attention because of his injury. During the exercises between classes, both Ms Zhang and Ms Guan Qi came to him. They looked at Little Auspicious's wound, which looked very strange, as it was just a small black spot. Little Auspicious pointed to it and said, 'It went through here.'

'Fortunately, there is no inflammation, and you didn't hit a bone!' said Ms Zhang.

Ms Guan patted Little Auspicious's head and said, 'This kid usually looks very delicate, but today's performance surprised me. He is still playing table tennis. It seems that he has grown up.'

Hearing what Ms Guan said, Little Auspicious was very happy. At that moment, he also felt that he was quite brave and strong.

CHAPTER TWENTY-THREE

Brother's Pigeon

It was spring in Beijing, and the sky was clear. Houses and yards were dilapidated. Green buds covered the branches of the jujube tree, and 'fart curtain' kites floated in the blue sky. The crab apple tree in front of the north house was just about to bloom, and each bud tightly held together, stirring people's hearts in anticipation. There was a sweet fragrance of flowers. From the next yard came the sound of someone playing with a diabolo, and the pleasant sound of buzzing moved far and near with the breeze.

Little Auspicious couldn't sit still any longer. He looked under the bed and found the diabolo that his mother had bought for him during the Chinese New Year. Then he ran to the yard, put the diabolo on the ground, and was about to shake the string off the stick when his brother rushed out. He didn't know which room he had come from.

Just then, Little Auspicious heard the whistle of pigeons floating in the air. He looked up to see a group of pigeons circling above. They were just black spots in the sky.

Big Auspicious opened the pigeon cage and then yelled loudly as if fighting a war. 'Heh-heh-heh!' The pigeons, some of which had been pecking on the ground while the others were resting in the cage, all rose into flight, filling the air with the sound of flapping wings. Little Auspicious's eyes were dazzled. Soon, the flock was flying in a circular route whose diameter was roughly the length of the alley.

Big Auspicious placed the wooden ladder against the courtyard wall. Little Auspicious stared blankly at his elder brother, who was focusing his eyes on the sky. Big Auspicious was reluctant to let his pigeons fly across such a large area. Little Auspicious understood that his brother wanted his pigeons to meet other pigeons in the distance.

Big Auspicious seemed to have eyes under his feet. He didn't look at the ladder at all. He jumped from the ladder to the courtyard wall and then ran along the top of the wall waving a short bamboo pole with a red cloth strip on the top. He wasn't looking where he was running. Little Auspicious was very worried. His brother's eyes were on the sky. What if he slipped and fell off the wall?

The sound of the diabolo stopped. There were shouts from other courtyards.

Little Auspicious saw another flock of pigeons flying towards the yard. His brother's pigeons also approached. For a while, the two groups of pigeons seemed a little confused. Big Auspicious was not as anxious as before. He was acting like a commander who had finished his first battle and was taking a break. He threw the short bamboo pole into the yard and began to clap softly. The sound from his mouth mimicked a pigeon beckoning home the birds.

Little Auspicious knew that his brother was using his pigeon hens to attract male pigeons. If they could be recruited, there would be a few more pigeons in the flock. Little Auspicious was nervous and excited.

The family's pigeons flew towards the courtyard. Big Auspicious jumped off the wall so that the male pigeons following, who could not resist the temptation of the hens, could fly down

without fear. Big Auspicious was like a hunter, standing in the yard looking at the sky anxiously but pretending to be calm.

Houses and yards belonged to each family, but there was only one blue sky. All the fun-loving people in the alley saw the scene in the sky. The gate of the courtyard opened, and both young and middle-aged people from outside rushed in, wanting to see the final result.

When Little Auspicious's brother had started raising pigeons, Little Auspicious was too young to remember anything. He heard from his mother that his elder brother had been diagnosed with heart disease when he was in the sixth grade at primary school. The doctor had said that he should not overexert himself and instead rest at home. Big Auspicious had taken a year off from school, and he had spent his days doing nothing. Old Li bought him a pair of pigeons to play with. Little Auspicious's brother had been a pigeon enthusiast ever since then.

Old Li bought the pigeons from the Huguo Temple Fair. Their father saw them when he got home, but he didn't say anything. Thus, Big Auspicious was given implicit permission to raise the pigeons. He placed the coops in the corridor. After having rested at home for more than half a year, Big Auspicious's heart had recovered. Their father said that if he was cured, the pigeons should be given away. Obediently, Big Auspicious gave the pigeons away.

But when his father left Beijing for work, Big Auspicious started raising pigeons again.

Two months later, when their father returned home, he saw the pigeon coop in the corridor. He didn't say anything.

The boys who were standing and cheering called out, 'Come down! Come down!'

Little Auspicious saw his brother's pigeons start to land, and several other pigeons from outside hovered over their yard. He imitated his brother's voice. 'Coo, coo, coo'. The excited children yelled and climbed up the rockery like monkeys. Big Auspicious didn't say a thing. He held a small basin in his left hand, scooped a large handful of sorghum rice from the basin with his right hand and threw it across the open space of the yard. Big Auspicious's pigeons landed on the ground, folded away their feathers, and pecked leisurely at the rice. The pigeons from outside, after hesitating, landed away from Big Auspicious and eyed their surroundings vigilantly.

This was the most critical moment of the battle. Big Auspicious had to use all his abilities to lead them, step by step, to a place where he could reach and capture them. The voices became quieter, and the atmosphere grew more tense.

'Little Auspicious! Push down the one next to the elm tree!' said his elder brother.

Hearing his brother's call, Little Auspicious was heartened. It was the first time his brother had trusted him like this.

There was a big elm tree at the corner of the rockery, and the pigeon, Iron Arm, stood on the top of the rockery. Little Auspicious picked up a piece of dirt and threw it towards the pigeon, and the broken dirt sprayed across the stone. The pigeon fluttered its wings, flew two or three metres and landed on another stone. These pigeons knew they were in danger, but they still refused to leave, which showed how much the hens and sorghum rice attracted them. The children who broke into the yard helped to scare the pigeons, herding them from the front to the back yard, where Big Auspicious quietly stood with a net.

Two foreign pigeons began to eat among the family pigeons. Big Auspicious held his breath, stooped, and walked over quietly, grabbing a foreign pigeon by the neck!

There were cheers in the courtyard.

No one noticed that Little Auspicious's father had returned home at this time. When Big Auspicious saw their father, it was already too late. Their father stood beside the rockery door near the backyard. Needless to say, he had seen the chaotic and lively scene in the courtyard.

Big Auspicious was stunned. His face turned pale. He held the net in his left hand and the pigeon in his right. The children standing on the rockery came down quietly and ran towards the gate. The yard immediately went quiet, except for the pigeons, who continued to peck at the sorghum rice on the ground, disregarding what was happening around them. Their father didn't seem to look at everything. He just stared coldly at Big Auspicious as he passed by, then he walked up the steps, took the cloth duster off the pillar, and slapped the dust off his shoes. The only sound in the whole yard came from the slapping of the cloth.

Big Auspicious and Little Auspicious both got into trouble. Little Auspicious had rarely seen his brother scared like this. Their dad's majesty was not in his loud scolding but in his stern silence.

Big Auspicious didn't eat dinner that evening. It wasn't their father's punishment; he went without of his own volition. He stood obediently in the corridor, hoping to obtain their father's forgiveness with such an attitude. Their father didn't stop him from eating but nor did he invite him to eat, and the family didn't mention it. This was the punishment Big Auspicious deserved. When their father was about to finish eating, he suddenly called Big Auspicious to eat. Big Auspicious sat down, a little flustered. After watching him finish his meal, their father said slowly, 'The pigeons can no longer be kept. The pigeon cage will be dismantled today. Will you dismantle it yourself, or shall I dismantle it for you?' Their father threw a vice at Big Auspicious's feet.

Big Auspicious was stunned. He may or may not have guessed what would happen, but this was undoubtedly the most severe punishment for him.

Big Auspicious looked into their father's eyes. 'Couldn't the cage be used to raise chickens?'

'No.'

'What about the pigeons?'

'All the pigeons will be released, and they will go to whoever's house they like.'

The sky was getting hazy. The pigeons made a 'coo-coo' sound. They didn't know that they couldn't live there anymore. Big Auspicious came to the corridor with his head down and started cutting the wires on the cage with pliers. The pigeons cooed in surprise, not knowing what was going on.

When the first crooked wire fell, Big Auspicious began to cry softly, and Little Auspicious also felt a little uncomfortable in his heart. But he knew that his father's mind could not be changed. All he heard was the 'click' of the pliers cutting the wires.

In the evening, Big Auspicious started to drive away his pigeons, but it was already late, and almost all the pigeons flapped their wings half-heartedly before landing on the ground again. Perhaps they thought *How can we fly in such a dark sky? Why can't we be accommodated in such a big yard?* Until late at night, there was still the sound of pigeons in the yard for a long, long time.

The next morning, Little Auspicious got up and ran to the yard. In the corridor was a small bundle of thick wire tied together. The pigeons were almost gone, except for two pacing pigeons on the top of the wall: Ink Ring and Iron Arm. They were looking at the yard. Maybe they wanted to come down and have a look.

Big Auspicious was not home. He had gone to school.

CHAPTER TWENTY-FOUR

Brother's Eagle

Little Auspicious was timid and relatively quiet, while his brother loved to play around. Big Auspicious and several friends would often go out of the city to catch grasshoppers and crickets, and they would often forget the time. On one occasion, the gates at Xizhimen and Fuchengmen were closed, so he and his friends had to stay outside the city overnight. In the early morning of the next day, after coming back into the city, he climbed up the power pole and dropped over the wall into the yard. Before he could enter the house, however, he was stopped by their father. Big Auspicious was made to kneel in the corridor for a whole hour.

Big Auspicious was not only mischievous but he also had many hobbies, especially performing Beijing opera. Because of this, Little Auspicious's family had a Beijing *hu*, an *erhu*, and a bamboo flute. The Beijing *hu* was loud and melodious and could create an atmosphere, but it was not easy to learn. If not played well, the sound was unsettling, similar to the noises a chicken makes when it is killed. Played well, it produced bright sounds that reflected the style of Beijing. The *erhu* was much more melodious and easier to learn. As the fingers of the left hand moved up and down the strings, the high and low notes would naturally appear as the right hand drew the bow across the strings. The inner strings were low-pitched and the outer strings high-pitched. It was not too difficult for most children to play a simple tune on the erhu after a while.

When he was in the third grade, Big Auspicious taught Little Auspicious how to play tunes on the erhu and the flute.

One day, Little Auspicious tried to play *The North Wind Blows* from *The White-haired Girl*, but his brother said, 'You're not playing it right.'

'What's wrong?' Little Auspicious suspected that his brother didn't want to teach him anymore.

'No rhythm.'

'What is "no rhythm"?'

While humming *The North Wind Blows*, Big Auspicious beat the tempo with his hands and asked Little Auspicious to follow suit. Little Auspicious followed, but he couldn't feel it. Regardless of how he tried tapping, he didn't feel like he was in harmony. Big Auspicious shook his head, turned around and left. As he left, he asked, 'Why is there so much rosin on the bow?'

In those days, the strings of the *erhu* were made of steel wire, and bows were made of horsehair. The horsehair was smeared with rosin. The friction that it created between the bow and the strings produced a loud sound. Big Auspicious was not happy when Little Auspicious used too much or too little rosin on the bow.

Once, his elder brother took him to watch a Beijing opera, *Iberham*, performed by two famous actors, Wu Suqiu and Jiang Tielin. In the play, they were lovers. They were also a couple in real life. When his brother told him this, Little Auspicious admired them even more. Wu Suqiu was beautiful, and Jiang Tielin was handsome. Little Auspicious also thought his brother was amazing and knew everything.

Their father often said with emotion, 'I don't understand. You can't study well. How can you become so addicted to raising pigeons and singing operas! If you put all your energy into studying, your homework would not be like this!'

Because no one in Little Auspicious's family knew how to manage the crab apple trees, they weren't pruned or fertilised. As a result, the crab apples it produced were small and astringent. But even so, they made the children salivate.

One autumn afternoon, some children from the alley came to Little Auspicious's house to play. They looked at the small white fruit on the tree and asked if they could have a taste. They wanted to know whether it was sour or sweet. Lao Dezi's sister immediately said, 'It doesn't matter if they are sour. Boil them in water and put in some sugar, and when the water is almost gone, it will stick. Candied crab apple!' What she said made everyone lick their lips. Little Auspicious climbed the tree. He saw his friends looking at him eagerly and gratefully, so he stepped on the branches more boldly to look for crab apples that he could reach.

Just then, the yard gate opened. Big Auspicious had returned from school. He had absolute authority over Little Auspicious.

He stood there, looked imperiously at Little Auspicious's group of friends, and shouted, 'Everyone, get out!' The children froze, like a group of puppets whose strings had been suddenly cut. After a moment of silence, the little friends ran out the gate despondently.

Big Auspicious went into the house, leaving Little Auspicious alone in the yard—he was still up the tree, and tears were streaming down his face.

Big Auspicious had a kite shaped like an eagle. When Beijingnese people speak about things, they often put 'old' in front of the word. An eagle flying in the sky is called 'an old eagle'.

Big Auspicious's old eagle kite was big. Its wingspan was wider than an adult's outstretched arms. The frame was made of bamboo, and the kite was painted in black and grey like a traditional Chinese painting. The eyes and beak were three-dimensional. Whether it was in the sky or hanging on a wall, the eagle looked bright and lifelike.

Big Auspicious's eagle was legendary. At that time, many kite-flying enthusiasts gathered in Shichahai, Beijing. His eagle was the only kite that could fly without any wind.

One day, Big Auspicious flew his kite in the yard. He let it fly very high, to such a height that no one would care about it, and it just flew freely in the blue sky. Big Auspicious tied the string of the kite to a pillar in the corridor and went into to the house. A short while later, he brought a long white paper with a small wire loop on top of the strip. He put the loop on the kite string and pushed it lightly with his hand. A miracle happened: Little Auspicious was surprised to see the long white strip being pulled up, as if by an invisible hand, floating along the kite line into the air, floating, floating, until finally the ribbon and eagle were one.

Little Auspicious looked at his brother with surprise. 'It's not difficult!' Big Auspicious said nonchalantly. At that moment, Little Auspicious really admired his brother.

The eagle kite was usually kept in a small storeroom full of sundries. One day, when his brother was out, Little Auspicious walked into the room alone to take a closer look at why the eagle was so magical. He touched the eagle's frame and then the hanging wings. Little Auspicious saw what looked like rat droppings under one of the wings. He picked them up. He noticed there was a small tear about a centimetre long towards the back hem of the wing. Little Auspicious was taken aback. He didn't dare linger anymore, so he hurried out the door.

Little Auspicious was terrified. That night his elder brother asked him, 'Did you move my kite?' Little Auspicious nodded and said, 'Yes, because there were rat droppings on it.' His brother glared angrily at him and then left. From that day on, Little Auspicious prepared for the arrival of a storm.

Little Auspicious tried to avoid his brother as much as possible. He didn't dare look at the eagle kite again, but he did want to know what had happened to the eagle.

His elder brother repaired the small tear with paper and traced over the wings with an ink pen.

Then, depressing news: the eagle could no longer fly when there was no wind. Little Auspicious wondered if such a big change could possibly have been caused by that little scar.

Then came news that when the eagle was released, it kept turning somersaults. Little Auspicious felt even more uneasy.

But his elder brother never lost his temper with Little Auspicious. He never flew the eagle kite again nor did he mention the matter again. The eagle kite remained quietly in the storeroom.

CHAPTER TWENTY-FIVE

Aunt Yu

It could have been that his father owed money. Or perhaps the family had no income. Little Auspicious didn't know. Whatever the reason, he rarely saw his father smile.

His father rented out another north room in the backyard. Originally, it had been a suite with access to the kitchen and bathroom through the hallway. Now, the outhouse was rented to someone else, so their father could only open a door between the back room and the kitchen.

That year, Little Auspicious's mother gave birth to a baby boy. The boy was a few months old when he contracted pneumonia. Little Auspicious's mother quickly took his baby brother to the hospital.

One evening, Little Auspicious was doing homework by the window. When his mother came back, his father asked, 'Where is the child?' Little Auspicious looked up. Unexpectedly, his mother said, 'He died in the hospital...' Before she could finish speaking, she fell on the bed and burst into tears.

Little Auspicious sat there. He watched his tears fall onto his homework book. He had no other way to comfort his mother, so he simply walked up to her and said, 'Mum, do not cry.'

His mother cried and said, 'It's all because the door between the back room and the kitchen was opened, and the northwest wind blew in. Your little brother caught a cold and died of pneumonia.'

After Little Auspicious's younger brother died, someone offered his mother a job looking after children. His mother took the job for two reasons. One was to ease her pain of losing a child, and the other was to increase the family's income. At that time, many revolutionary cadres went to the city. National cadres had a fixed salary, but they were very busy with their work, and they had to find someone to help them look after their children.

The baby was a little girl named Xiaoqing. Both her parents were in their thirties, and they were overjoyed to have this child, who was very precious to them. Xiaoqing's parents were very polite to Little Auspicious's mother, and they were also very kind. This was Little Auspicious's first encounter with people from Shanxi, who spoke very differently from the Shandong people. Whereas people from Shandong speak thickly and honestly, people from Shanxi speak delicately as if they are negotiating on good terms.

On one of the walls in Little Auspicious's house was an old painting inlaid with glass. *Drinking Horses* depicted horses drinking water from a river. Some people were standing, and others were sleeping peacefully. Little Auspicious didn't know if the painting was worth anything, but he once heard from his brother that *Cabbage*, a painting by Qi Baishi, a modern ink painting master painter, had recently been sold by an art shop for only eighteen yuan. Maybe other people wouldn't even want their painting at home.

There was a new picture hanging next to the picture of the horses. It was the promotional picture *Peace Dove*, and it had been bought by Xiaoqing's parents. In the painting, a chubby little boy was lying down with his head and hands raised. In front of him was a white dove. Little Auspicious noticed that the artist's name was Jiang Zhaohe.

Aunt Yu lived in the room separated from the north room. Aunt Yu's husband had passed away, and she had come to Beijing from the northeast with her three daughters. The eldest daughter was married, and the second and youngest daughters lived with Aunt Yu. The youngest daughter was three years older than Little Auspicious, and they would play together occasionally. Aunt Yu was very forthright and lively. She had a gramophone and almost always played the same record. The lyrics from that record always lingered in Little Auspicious's mind:

> Brother, don't forget me! I am your dear Mei Niang...

There were mulberry trees in the front yard and backyard of Little Auspicious's house. His father once pointed to the bark of the mulberry tree and said to Little Auspicious, 'Look, the bark of the mulberry tree splits as it grows. Why? Once upon a time, when Zhu Yuanzhang was not the emperor, on the way to escape, he was in a remote area, thirsty and hungry. Suddenly he saw a mulberry tree. He gobbled up the mulberries. They were really delicious! He said to the mulberry tree, "One day, I will become the emperor, and I will make you the king of trees!" The mulberry tree heard this and was very happy. Later, Zhu Yuanzhang became the emperor. One day, he saw an ailanthus tree, which looked similar to a mulberry tree. He remembered the mulberry tree that had saved his life, and he remembered the promise he had made back then. He pointed to the ailanthus tree and said, "I will make you the king of trees!" The emperor's words were golden. From then on, the ailanthus tree grew fast and strong. But the mulberry tree, what about it? He was angry in his heart, and his stomach burst out of anger.'

Little Auspicious listened with great interest. The next time he saw mulberry trees, he felt that they looked a little pitiful.

His father could tell stories about mulberry trees, but he didn't see the usefulness of mulberry trees. He had two mulberry trees, but he didn't raise silkworms. Aunt Yu saw the opportunity, and she started to raise silkworms as a serious undertaking. Little Auspicious often went to her house to watch the growth of those little creatures. There were many densely packed black dots on a piece of paper. They were silkworms! She sprayed water on them and then covered them with a quilt. After a few days, small silkworms would come out, small and black, like punctuation marks. In a few more days, the silkworms would turn white and grow bigger, and it would be time to feed them mulberry leaves. The sound of the silkworms eating the leaves was very pleasant: 'Sha sha sha sha'. Little Auspicious watched them grow into big silkworms and then gradually turn golden yellow, spin silk and form cocoons, turning themselves into pupae. One day, the pupae in the cocoons turned into little moths. They bit through their cocoons and crawled out of them.

In those few days, hundreds of small pink and white moths flapped their wings and fell on top of a big bamboo basket as if they were holding a meeting to celebrate their victory. Aunt Yu put the basket on the table. Little Auspicious and his mother stood aside and watched. Some moths had other moths attached to their tails. Little Auspicious asked curiously, 'What are they doing?' Aunt Yu laughed heartily. 'They are getting married! If they don't get married, they won't have children. Then how can there be more silkworms next year?' Little Auspicious's face suddenly turned red. Aunt Yu laughed again. 'This child is blushing!'

When the silkworms made cocoons, Little Auspicious got them to produce their silk onto a round piece of paper. The silk on the paper became thicker and thicker. He then put this thick and soft silk into an ink cartridge and poured a little ink onto it. This was his cartridge. He no longer had to bring an ink bottle to calligraphy class.

CHAPTER TWENTY-SIX

Parachute

Beijing has four distinct seasons. In the winter, it snows. Beijing's snow has a temper – either no snow falls or it is very imposing and heavy snow. When it snows, the snowflakes fly, and no one can see more than four or five metres. If it snowed overnight, the yard next morning would be covered with ankle-deep silvery-white snow. The snow would make a creaking sound when it was stepped on.

If Little Auspicious needed to go to school during those days, his mother would put a white cloth bag over Little Auspicious. When he got to school, he would just shake the bag to get the snow off.

It was a common thing to have snowball fights and make snowmen. All the tree branches were beautifully decorated with white snow. A mischievous classmate deliberately called Little Auspicious over to a tree as if to tell him a secret. When he arrived, the classmate kicked the tree trunk with his foot, and snow fell like a shower of petals on Little Auspicious. The classmate ran away with a smile. When Little Auspicious read 'Thousands of trees and thousands of pear blossoms', he felt that the poet wrote well and that his writing was just like what he had seen!

Once, when it was snowing, Little Auspicious's father read a poem to him: 'The world is one, the well is black, the yellow dog turns into a white dog, and the white dog is swollen.' Little Auspicious thought it was very funny. His father said, 'Write it down on paper tonight.' That evening, Little Auspicious wrote, *There is a bucket in the sky, a black hole in the well, a black dog becomes a white dog, and a white dog becomes a fat dog*. His father compared it with the original. Little Auspicious had made a lot of mistakes. Not only did his father not criticise him but he also even patted his head and said, 'Not bad, not bad, especially the last sentence.'

In summer, of course, it rained, and when it did, the rain was heavy.

Little Auspicious didn't like to go to school when it rained. He didn't have rain boots. His mother made him wear a pair of worn-out cloth shoes to school. He didn't have a good umbrella, so he had to take a broken one. At that time, there were only two kinds of umbrellas. One was made of oilcloth. There was only one of those at home, and the adults would use it when they went out. There was also a kind of paper umbrella which had a bamboo frame with kraft paper pasted onto it. The paper was then coated with tung oil. This kind of umbrella was easy to break, and the circle would often turn into a half-circle when it was opened. Little Auspicious used this kind of umbrella when he went to school. If it rained heavily, he was made to wear the white bag. Little Auspicious felt very humiliated and ashamed to have to wear broken shoes and use a broken umbrella.

Little Auspicious also had many troubles with the clothes he wore.

One day, his mother made him a new shirt. It was white with long sleeves. It was very white, and the fabric was very strong! At first glance, the material appeared to be either silk or satin, and the cloth had a faint lustre. His mother told him, 'This shirt has been made out of a parachute.'

Parachute – the real parachute that a pilot uses when ejecting from a plane, of course! Creamy white, soft, slippery to the touch.

The texture of the parachute cloth had made it very difficult to sew. The fabric was so strong that it could not be torn, and it was impossible to cut a straight line in it with scissors. Little Auspicious's mother was very smart. She had first cut out the shapes for the shirt from cardboard and then glued the parachute cloth to the cardboard. After the glue had dried, she cut it out the shapes, then soaked them in water and separated the cloth from the cardboard. His mother then sewed the pieces of fabric together to make Little Auspicious's shirt.

Little Auspicious was an honest and obedient child, so he went to school in clothes made of parachutes.

No one noticed his new shirt when he entered school in the morning, but Little Auspicious was acutely aware of it. The shirt was airtight, uncomfortable to wear, and a little tight. Little Auspicious comforted himself. *Maybe it just feels like this because it is the first time, I'm wearing it.*

During the exercise between classes, the other students noticed the shirt, but they didn't admire it or envy Little Auspicious. They were simply curious.

The students touched it and asked, 'What kind of cloth is this made of? It's soft and slippery.'

'It has been made from a parachute,' Little Auspicious said, unconfidently.

'Stop bragging! Where did you get the parachute?'

It's a parachute. Our family has a parachute!' Little Auspicious said.

‘What’s so great about a parachute? We still have an aeroplane at home!’ Pu Yunsheng bragged sarcastically, making it seem that Little Auspicious had also been bragging.

Mr Lian, a history teacher, came over. Mr Lian was thin and wore glasses. No one knew why the teachers called him ‘Mr Lian’, which was a more sincere title than ‘Teacher Lian’. The students also called him ‘Mr Lian’.

Mr Lian looked at Little Auspicious’s shirt and asked, ‘What type of thread did your mother use to sew this?’

‘Just ordinary thread.’

The students stopped talking and looked at Mr Lian.

‘It really is made of parachute cloth.’ Mr Lian twisted Little Auspicious’s sleeve with his hands and asked, ‘Can you ask your mother how it was cut?’

Little Auspicious looked at the classmates around him. No one spoke. He was very proud. Mr Lian asked again, ‘Where did your parachute come from?’

Little Auspicious shook his head. Mr Lian didn’t ask any more questions.

In the second class of the afternoon, Little Auspicious’s class had a history lesson with Mr Lian. As soon as Mr Lian arrived, he said, ‘Today, I will tell you the story of the parachute.’

The students raised their heads and looked at Mr Lian intently. Several students looked at Little Auspicious’s shirt. Little Auspicious couldn’t wait to take in every word the teacher was going to say.

Mr Lian said, ‘During the Anti-Japanese War, I went to school in Kunming. We were close to the Kunming Central Aviation School, where our pilots were trained. Today, I saw student Little Auspicious wearing a shirt made of parachute fabric. It reminds me of a story about two heroes that is related to parachutes.’

The students stopped talking.

'China's Anti-Japanese War was tragic, and the story of what happened to the Chinese Air Force during the Anti-Japanese War was also tragic. We must always remember them.' Pausing for a moment, Mr Lian cleared his throat.

'There was a young man from Guangdong named Ye Pengfei. At that time, China's aircraft lacked parts and maintenance personnel, and they often broke down. Ye Pengfei actually experienced two failures in the air. Both times, he had no choice but to eject. He survived, but both planes were destroyed. Ye Pengfei was very sad, and he felt ashamed to see others. He vowed he would never eject again. But fate seemed to be against him. While returning to the airfield after a scouting flight, his plane suffered a serious failure. His superior ordered him to eject, but he did not obey. Instead, he remained in the plane as it crashed to the ground.'

'There was also a young man named Lin Yao who fought as a pilot against the Japanese. During one mission, his plane suffered damage, and Lin Yao had to eject. Unfortunately, his parachute didn't open, and Lin Yao fell to his death. When Lin Yao's unopened parachute was rolled out, everyone couldn't help but lie on the parachute, crying.'

Mr Lian was very emotional. He pointed to Little Auspicious's shirt and said loudly, 'This shirt worn by your classmate may have been carried by some heroes. They may have fought many battles! The material may appear to be just cloth made of silk or nylon. But, in fact, parachutes represent hope, heroes and glory.'

The classroom was very quiet, apart from a girl crying softly at the back. Mr Lian finished speaking. Little Auspicious's face and ears felt hot. He felt as if his shirt were filled with the wind, and his body seemed to be floating. He had heard that a distant relative of the family had been a pilot and had done meritorious service in the Anti-Japanese War. Little Auspicious's shirt must have come from his relative's parachute. That's right! Little Auspicious was very proud of having figured it out.

Little Auspicious heard from the other teachers that during the Anti-Japanese War, Mr Lian was a student at Southwest Associated University.

For the next two days, Little Auspicious wore his parachute shirt everywhere. He felt very honoured, even though the shirt was airtight and made him uncomfortable. When someone asked him where the parachute had come from, he told them it had belonged to his distant relative, who was a pilot in the Anti-Japanese War. He felt that his classmates envied him. After three days, his mother asked him to take off his shirt and wash it.

Little Auspicious asked her, 'Where did our parachute come from?'

'I can't explain it to you. You are too young!'

'I am not young! I understand! Did our relative stay here? He was a pilot, wasn't he?' Little Auspicious was in high spirits.

Just then, his father walked in and asked Little Auspicious's mother, 'What is this about a pilot?'

'Little Auspicious asked where the parachute came from.'

His father was stunned for a moment and whispered, 'Little Auspicious, don't tell outsiders that there are parachutes in our family. Do you understand?'

Seeing his father's serious eyes, Little Auspicious nodded. He vaguely felt that their relative, a pilot, was not something that should be talked about publicly, but how could Mr Lian talk about it in class?

His father said, 'I'll tell you where our parachute came from.'

Little Auspicious hadn't wanted to ask about the parachute anymore, but now that his father offered to explain, Little Auspicious was very happy.

'I bought this parachute at the market,' his father said flatly.

Little Auspicious was very disappointed. But Big Auspicious kept winking at Little Auspicious, and he knew he couldn't ask any more questions.

The next day, when Little Auspicious was alone with his elder brother, Big Auspicious told him, 'Papa bought this, but not at the market.'

Little Auspicious was very surprised. 'Did he buy it in a store?'

His brother shook his head. 'Let me tell you. When the Japanese devils surrendered, the supplies left by their army belonged to China. Some of the things were auctioned. Father participated in an auction and bought enough things to fill two houses!'

'Ah! Were they all parachutes?'

'No. They had everything! He bought Japanese military uniforms, Go games, skates, cooking utensils, sweaters and trousers, as well as typewriters and notebooks for printing. And parachutes!'

'Where are those things?'

'Why would our family want these things? Dad found people who needed these things and sold them to them. He wanted to make some money. In the end, the money he got back was less than the money he spent, so he lost. The family only has a few bits and pieces left.'

Little Auspicious understood that his shirt was made of leftover parachute cloth.

'Do you understand?' his brother asked.

Little Auspicious nodded. He felt that his parachute was not as glorious as the parachute that the teacher had talked about. So, he asked again, 'Did our relative not have a parachute?'

'Yes, but you can't take anything home!' Big Auspicious shook his head.

Little Auspicious was suddenly discouraged. This was a parachute that had belonged to the Japanese devils. It was not an honourable thing at all.

His elder brother seemed to see his thoughts. He patted him on the shoulder and said, 'It's an honour to use the spoils of war from defeating the Japanese devils to make clothes!'

Finally, Big Auspicious said, 'You must not tell anybody what I've told you!'

The next day, Little Auspicious said to his mother, 'Mum, I don't want to wear this shirt anymore. It's not breathable.'

'What's the matter? You liked it so much two days ago that you didn't even want to take it off.'

'I don't want to wear it anymore. Once it gets wet or I sweat, people can see my skin, and it looks ugly!'

His mother sighed. 'Do you know how difficult it was for me to make this shirt for you?'

Little Auspicious said, 'I know you worked hard on it, but it is not comfortable to wear. It neither absorbs sweat nor breathes!'

His mother sighed and said nothing more.

A Team Day was coming up at school, and the students were required to wear a white sweatshirt and blue trousers. Little Auspicious didn't have a white sweatshirt, so his mother asked him to wear the parachute shirt.

Little Auspicious suddenly remembered the two yuan he had saved, which was the fortune money given by his relatives during the Spring Festival, which his mother had not taken. She told Little Auspicious that he should save it to buy a new umbrella. Little Auspicious said, 'I will use the money I saved to buy white cloth, and you can make me a shirt.'

His mother got angry. 'Isn't that the money for the umbrella?'

'Let's make sweatshirts first!'

‘The older you get, the more demanding you become, and you now give orders to your mum!” His mother was furious and slapped him on the buttocks. ‘The bigger you are, the more ignorant you become!’

Little Auspicious was rarely beaten and even more rarely scolded.

Little Auspicious walked into the yard and hid under the big elm tree at the corner of the rockery. Just then, Mr Lao, who lived in the front yard, happened to come out. He saw Little Auspicious and walked over slowly, and asked him what was going on. Little Auspicious explained what had happened.

The next night, his mother bought a piece of bleached white cloth and started making a new shirt for Little Auspicious. Little Auspicious knew that it was not easy for his mother to do so. He felt very ashamed and put the two yuan in his mother's hand. His mother put away the money, and Little Auspicious felt a little more at ease.

A week later, Little Auspicious was called to Mr Lao's house. Mr Lao handed him an umbrella.

The frame of the umbrella appeared to Little Auspicious to be made of aluminium, and it was very light in his hand. When the umbrella opened, the tightly stretched fabric was milky white with a slight lustre. It looked familiar to Little Auspicious. For a while, he couldn't remember where he had seen it.

‘It was made from your parachute shirt,’ said Mr Lao.

‘Parachute!’ Little Auspicious was surprised and delighted. He saw the regular machine-made stitches on the umbrella, which turned the shirt into a round umbrella surface. The old man had changed the shirt made from a parachute into an umbrella!

‘There is no other such umbrella in the whole world,’ Mr Lao claimed proudly.

Little Auspicious was too surprised to speak.

'Take it!'

Since then, when it rained, Little Auspicious had a high-grade umbrella of his own! It was translucent, and it was not breathable or water-absorbent.

One day, Little Auspicious suddenly wondered, when did Mr Lao get the parachute shirt from his mother? Most probably, the Elder Ms Lao had talked to his mother.

CHAPTER TWENTY-SEVEN

Red Star Drawing Pin Commune

In later years, Little South House was no longer used to accommodate guests. It was converted to a multi-purpose room. In front of the window near the east gate of the courtyard, there was an amber yellow double-sided desk where Little Auspicious's father would often practise calligraphy. On the other side of the house were drill presses, paint buckets and piles of miscellaneous machine parts.

Little Auspicious's father and several of his friends jointly opened a toy factory, specialising in making wooden toys such as cars, small cranes and tractors. Little South House became the factory's temporary office, and Little Auspicious's home became a part of the toy factory.

Unpainted wooden toy parts began to appear in the yard of Little Auspicious's house, including small wheels the size of persimmon cakes. They were still very rough, and the burrs on them were still prickly. One day, Little Auspicious helped the adults smooth these wheels with sandpaper. First, they put putty on the wheel. Then, when it dried, they sanded it with coarse sandpaper and then finished it off with fine sandpaper.

The yard was filled with a strong smell of paint after workers sprayed the polished toy parts with paint. One day, trucks came and took away all the toy parts, as well as the miscellaneous machines at Little South House. Little Auspicious heard from his mother that his father had had an argument with his partners, and the toy factory couldn't continue, so they had to close the business. The family was in debt again.

One day, Little Auspicious came home from school and saw stacks of wooden boards in the yard. His father used them to lay a new floor in the Little South House. There was no basement. The planks were laid on top of grey bricks. The new floor was messy and unsightly, and it flexed when people walked on it.

His father was not a businessman. He had studied at a military academy and served as a soldier. He could write beautiful calligraphy. No one imagined that he would start making tofu in Little South House.

Little South House was converted into a tofu shop. Little Auspicious's father opened a window on the side facing the street so that he could sell tofu from it.

He didn't know how to make tofu, so he employed two masters who made tofu. Little Auspicious often came to Little South House to watch them cook the soybeans and then grind them in a stone mill to produce soybean milk. When the soybean milk boiled, it was poured through a thick layer of gauze into a large drawer surrounded by four pieces of bamboo. At this stage, it was still a free-flowing liquid. A bowl of brine was added to it, then it was covered with gauze and placed inside a wooden square, then pressed down with a stone, the liquid would flow down the edge of the bamboo drawer. After an hour's work, the drawer cloth was lifted up to reveal white tofu!

When Little South House began selling tofu through the window to the street, the people in the alley were surprised. How could the owner sell tofu from such a beautiful and large yard?

One would only know their own family's bitterness! As the saying goes, every family has its own hard-to-recite sayings.

Unfortunately, the tofu shop was open for less than two months. Little Auspicious's father said that in those two months, the only benefit their family gained was eating tofu without spending money.

The window facing the street in Little South House was bricked up, and the courtyard of Little Auspicious's house regained its mysterious appearance. His father registered a small business called 'Red Star Family Drawing Pin Commune'. Little Auspicious's father started making drawing pins, and Little South House turned into a small factory again.

Little South House was as big as two bungalows. Machines for making drawing pins were installed in it. Little Auspicious would often hear terms such as 'tamper' and 'curium'. A small nail would be placed into a lower mould. A small round metal disc was placed in an upper mould, then the two moulds were pressed together, integrating the disc with the nail, forming a drawing pin. The tamper was the main part of the machine. The curium was a mould that was placed on the hammer, and the heavy wheel above it was turned down hard until the curium hit the drawing pin and gave it its final shape.

There were three workers in the Drawing Pin Commune. One was a cousin who had just returned from the war to resist American aggression and aid Korea. The other two were Little Auspicious's father and sister. His elder sister had a hard life. Her education ended after she graduated from junior high school, and she then began working to help support the family.

(Big Auspicious had gone to work in a military factory in Baotou. Details about the factory were kept secret. Letters from the family had to be addressed to a mailbox numbered '××'. Later, when the family discovered that the factory where Big Auspicious worked manufactured tanks, they felt very proud.)

Little Auspicious's sister was the main force in manufacturing the drawing pins. They looked simple – just a cap and a nail – but they were difficult to make. Much sweat and tears – and also his sister's blood – went into making the pins. The fifteen-year-old girl was not only the main force but also the Drawing Pin Commune's salesperson! The family worked hard for a month to produce about a hundred small boxes of drawing pins. Then they packed them in a small wooden box and sent them to the place where they were purchased. The purchasers were very strict; they would open a box of drawing pins, and if any were rusty or if their shells weren't glossy, they wouldn't buy them.

Why did they send his sister sell the pins? The reason was obvious. She was a girl; people would be more sympathetic and considerate. It would be more difficult if an older man went there; they simply would not buy the pins. If that were the case, one month's labour would turn into tears for the whole family.

Every time Little Auspicious's sister left the courtyard on a tricycle with a box of drawing pins, their father looked nervous. He knew that the likelihood of success was fifty-fifty. Little Auspicious's elder sister carried the hopes of the whole family and the anxiety of their father, just like a soldier embarking on a journey.

Every time Little Auspicious's sister went to sell drawing pins, Old Li helped to pull the tricycle. On that day, he dressed neatly and borrowed a tricycle. Old Li said, 'Every penny saved is a penny earned.'

The process of manufacturing the drawing pins was semi-mechanised. *Place the small metal disc on the nail with your left hand and then remove your hand immediately; turn the wheel with your right hand to bring the mould down.* If your left hand were still there, it would be injured.

Performing thousands of such repetitive operations a day inevitably led to accidents. One day, his sister's hand was caught in the machine. Their father took her to the hospital. They saved her hand, but half of her little finger was missing. Every time Little Auspicious saw his sister's finger, he felt very sad. The whole family felt sorry for her.

His sister's hand was still wrapped in gauze when she went to sell the finished drawing pins. That day Little Auspicious was relaxed. He felt that the buyer would not make things difficult for her and would definitely accept all of the pins. *Sister's hand has been injured. Why don't you buy the pins?*

With the arrival of the national handicraft cooperative movement, the family's drawing pin company was merged with an instrument factory. The new factory was in the outer suburbs of Beijing. Little Auspicious's cousin went to the factory, and his father also went to the factory, returning home only once a week. Little South House changed from a workshop back to a dwelling.

CHAPTER TWENTY-EIGHT

Lying Flower

Little Auspicious's sister didn't go to the factory in the suburbs. Instead, she got married, in the year that Little Auspicious was in the fifth grade of primary school.

A few days before his sister's wedding, their father took Little Auspicious to Tongheju, a Shandong-style restaurant in Xisi Pailou, to order food for the wedding. His father asked Little Auspicious to pick a dish. Little Auspicious picked fried meatballs. But the manager said, 'Fried meatballs are not fit for such a banquet.' Little Auspicious's father smiled and said, 'It doesn't matter. If Little Auspicious likes fried meatballs, then we will order fried meatballs.'

The Elder Ms Lao attended his sister's wedding on behalf of her family. She drank too much that night, so Old Li took her home by rickshaw. She entered the yard, then took a few steps before collapsing in the courtyard in front of the steps. On the left side of the corridor were two large fish tanks full of water lilies, and on the right was a beautiful rose garden. Now that their flowers had faded, the trees were full of thick leaves.

Little Auspicious and his parents came out and hurried to her side. 'Are you all right?'

'It's okay. It's not a problem for me.' The Elder Ms Lao smiled and waved her hand. 'Let Little Auspicious stay with me for a while.'

Little Auspicious squatted down. He was very happy to receive such attention.

'I'm not angry that your sister got married. I'm very happy,' said the Elder Ms Lao.

'No one said you were angry,' said Little Auspicious's mother.

They tried to persuade her to go into the house to rest. It was October, late autumn, and it was getting cold. The sky was very clear, and the moon was bright.

'I'm not going inside. I want to stay here and look at the moon.' No one could change her mind, so the Second Ms Lao brought a coat from the house and tried to put it on her. But the Elder Ms Lao swatted the coat to the floor.

Little Auspicious's father came over and squatted down next to her. 'It will be fine in a while, don't worry. Little Auspicious, sing *Little Son-in-Law* for Auntie.'

'I don't want to listen to *Little Son-in-Law*!' the Elder Ms Lao protested, grabbing Little Auspicious's hand. Seeing that, his father said, 'Little Auspicious, you can stay here with the Elder Aunt Lao.'

The Second Ms Lao said, 'Little Auspicious, look after her. I'll go and pour some vinegar for her to sober up.' Then everyone left, leaving Little Auspicious sitting on the steps with the Elder Ms Lao.

'Little Auspicious, do you know that there is only one moon in the whole world?' the Elder Ms Lao asked quietly. Little Auspicious nodded. What she said was true, but Little Auspicious still felt it was a strange thing to say.

Then the Elder Ms Lao suddenly burst into tears. Little Auspicious didn't know what to do.

'Do you know this poem? "The moon rises above the sea, and the sky is with us sharing the moment..."' Little Auspicious was confused by the Elder Ms Lao's seemingly random words.

Little Auspicious shook his head.

'Don't get the word "rise" wrong,' said Little Auspicious, mistakenly thinking that the word should be 'raise' instead of 'rise'.

'Little Auspicious, I'm not angry that your sister got married, and I'm not jealous, because I also had a boyfriend. He was younger than me; he was a captain, and he was very handsome! He wanted to go to Qingdao. I told him not to go, but he insisted on going. He said he would come back in a day or two. Then he left and went to Taiwan, and he never came back. He said, "a day or two", but two or three years have passed.' The Elder Ms Lao cried again.

Little Auspicious was stunned. The Elder Ms Lao had said that she had a boyfriend! He was a captain, and he went to Taiwan. There was always a vaguely worrying feeling when talking about Taiwan. If someone in the family was in Taiwan, it was assumed to be a bad thing.

Little Auspicious looked around. There was no one around. The moon shone brightly. He tried to sound like an adult. 'It's okay. It will be fine soon.'

'At first, I thought that the relationship would bloom and bear fruit. I later realised that some flowers bloom but don't bear fruit. That kind of flower is a lying flower!'

The next morning, Little Auspicious woke up still a little confused. He couldn't remember when he had been brought inside. Perhaps he had fallen asleep beside the Elder Ms Lao.

He saw the Elder Ms Lao again at noon. She looked okay. No one would have guessed she had been drunk the night before.

'Little Auspicious, were you with me last night? In the yard?'

Little Auspicious nodded.

'What did I say?'

Little Auspicious replied instinctively. 'Nothing.'

'Did I say something when I was drunk?'

Little Auspicious shook his head.

The Elder Ms Lao asked again, 'Didn't I say anything?'

Little Auspicious thought for a while, then he said, 'You recited a poem.'

The Elder Ms Lao was stunned for a moment. Then she looked into Little Auspicious's eyes and asked him in a serious voice, 'What poem?'

'"The moon rises above the sea, and the sky is with us sharing the moment."'

'What else?'

Little Auspicious shook his head. His intuition told him not to tell the Elder Ms Lao that she had spoken about her boyfriend, because that would make her sad and upset. Little Auspicious loved her and knew she would not want others to know her secret. He wanted to comfort her, so he said, 'There really wasn't anything else.'

Little Auspicious felt that he had done a very kind thing. He also felt grown-up because he knew a secret he hadn't told anyone.

CHAPTER TWENTY-NINE

Picture Book Bookstore

Of all his classmates, Liu Guangting was the one with whom Little Auspicious had the best relationship. Little Auspicious and many of his classmates didn't have a radio at home, but Liu Guangting did. He lived in Xiaocheng Alley, so Little Auspicious often went to his house after school to listen to the chatterbox. It was a simple radio, containing only three vacuum tubes.

In those days, a radio needed an antenna and a ground wire. One end of the antenna was connected to the radio, and the other was held above the roof with a wooden pole or a bamboo pole. The antennae looked like spiders' webs or noodles and dumplings. The ground wire connected the radio to an iron earthing rod inserted into the ground. Many houses had brick or earth floors, which made it easy to install earthing rods.

The most popular shows were the *Little Trumpet* programme of the Central People's Broadcasting Station and the storytelling programme by Lian Kuoru. The chatterbox would sometimes crack and whine as Liu Guangting and Little Auspicious were listening. When this happened Liu Guangting's father would bring a kettle and pour water into the place where the tongs were inserted into the radio boosting the signal. When

600 700 800 1000 1200 1400 1600
500 400 300 250 200
4 5 6 7 8 10 12
75 60 50 37 30 25

this was done, the sound of the radio would become much clearer. The boys didn't why this worked, but they learned later that the water improved the conductivity of the connection, thus enhancing the effect of the ground wire.

Besides listening to the radio, everyone's favourite thing to do was read picture books. At the north corner of the eastern entrance to Dacheng Alley, there was a picture book bookstore. The door of the Little People's Bookstore opened towards the much wider Zhaodengyu Road. Sigengbai Primary School was diagonally opposite. Many children came to the bookstore to read books every day. Little Auspicious was also a frequent visitor.

The bookstore was a bungalow of ten square metres. The owner was a middle-aged man named Tan. He was very mysterious. When a new picture book came in, he would tear off the cover and replace it with kraft paper, sewing it on firmly with thread. Then Boss Tan began to show his skills. His calligraphy was very good. Little Auspicious would often wonder if that was why he changed the book covers.

Boss Tan glued the book covers that he had torn off onto a large piece of paper and hung it on the wall. As soon as the children came in, they would see the colourful covers of the new books and would ask for them. Then Boss Tan would go to the shelf and get the books for them.

Ordinary children's books could be rented for one cent and thicker ones for two cents. After paying the money and taking the book, a child could then sit on a small stool to read it.

Just inside the entrance to the bookstore, there were two rows of small benches on the left and right. When the store was full and the weather was good, Boss Tan would put out some small stools by the door.

Little Auspicious read many books there. Most of them were martial arts novels and folk tales, such as *Peng Gong An*,

Shi Gong An, and *The Seven Heroes and Five Gallants*. He also read picture books adapted from classic literature, such as *Three Kingdoms*, *Water Margin* and *Journey to the West*.

Little Auspicious liked to show off to others after reading books. When he retold to others the stories he had read, he was very satisfied when they praised him. This is how he earned himself the nickname 'Big Talk Auspicious'.

The young heroes in the books were his favourites: Zhao Yun (courtesy name: Zhao Zilong) in *The Romance of the Three Kingdoms*; the young Luo Cheng (courtesy name: Luo Gongran) in *The Romance of the Sui and Tang Dynasties*; and Zhan Zhao (courtesy name: Zhan Xiongfei) in *The Seven Heroes and Five Gallants*. It was so exciting for Little Auspicious to recite the heroes' names alongside their courtesy names.

To rent a book cost one cent, which may seem cheap at first glance, but it was difficult for ordinary children to be able to read two or three books at the store. At that time, children often bought vinegar for two cents and soy sauce for three cents in grocery stores. Little Auspicious's family gave him about thirty cents a month as pocket money. To Little Auspicious, reading children's books was enjoyable and addictive, but he never had enough money to read as much as he would have liked to. Only when he grew up did Little Auspicious understand that there were many other benefits in reading books.

The students found many different ways to spend less money and read more books. The techniques varied from person to person. Two students would rent separate books and then exchange them after finishing them. If Boss Tan saw them doing that, he would scold them. Another way was to have one person reading in between two others; this way, three people could read the same book. However, this was also not allowed by Boss Tan. These two methods were favoured by students who were more courageous and thick-skinned.

It was unknown who came up with the idea of renting a book then sitting on a stool outside the door next to three or four classmates, all of them sitting where Boss Tan couldn't see them. When he came out, they would stand up. The student who had rented the book would read it aloud while the others listened and occasionally glanced at the book. They had good eyesight, and a distance of one metre was no trouble for them. The other students around admired the reader. Of course, everyone wanted to play the reader's role.

At school, each class was divided into several study groups. Those whose lived closest to each other formed a group of three or four people. Some were better at studying, while others struggled. There were four people in Little Auspicious's study group. The other members were Song Xiaohui, Liu Guangting, and Pu Yunsheng. After finishing their homework, the four of them would often go to read books at the Little People's Bookstore.

One day, Little Auspicious rented two picture books for two cents and then went to the door. Pu Yunsheng said, 'Song Xiaohui is good at reading aloud, so let her read it.' Little Auspicious was stunned for a moment. Without hesitation, Song Xiaohui picked up a book, sat on a stool and began to read.

Song Xiaohui was very good-looking. She was often called upon to recite passages in class and selected when the school chose students to participate in extracurricular activities. She was the one who went to the radio station to introduce how foreign children collected stamps, even though she did not even collect stamps.

Song Xiaohui read expressively: 'Golden conch...' Little Auspicious was very upset. Why did all the good things to Song Xiaohui? He had paid for the books, but she just sat there confidently and read. Although he was upset, Little Auspicious was too embarrassed to express it. He didn't want to complain. Instead, he kept coughing and walking back and forth. Liu Guangting didn't recognize Little Auspicious's annoyance. He said, 'Be quiet, please!'

After finishing the first book, Song Xiaohui reached out for the second book, but Little Auspicious couldn't help it anymore. He didn't speak. He just sat on his stool with the book in his hands. His mind was so confused that, for a moment, he didn't know what was written on the first page.

'Read!' said Pu Yunsheng.

'I don't want to read,' Little Auspicious said angrily.

The other three students looked at each other, not knowing what had happened. They could see Little Auspicious's unwillingness.

At this moment, Boss Tan walked out of the shop. The children were a little nervous.

'Are you taking advantage again?' asked Boss Tan.

Song Xiaohui was ruthless. 'How are we taking advantage? We read it alone, and the others listen. Does it cost money to listen? You listen to the chatterbox every day. Have you paid the radio station yet?'

Boss Tan was calm. 'Why are you so unreasonable, little girl? Instead, you think of *me* as unreasonable! I am glad you read the book, but do you all know what it says in the book?'

'Of course, I know!' Liu Guangting and Pu Yunsheng said together.

'Have you read *Water Margin*?'

'I've read it. A hundred and eight heroes in *Water Margin*. Who doesn't know it?' They echoed.

Mr Tan straightened his scarf and said, 'Okay, today I will make a bet with you. If any of you can recite all one hundred and eight names and nicknames of the heroes, I will let you read twenty books for free! If you can't, then you can't read like this anymore.'

Everyone but Little Auspicious was stunned. Reciting ten, twenty, or even thirty names would have been okay, but it was too difficult to remember and recite a hundred and eight of them! But Little Auspicious's heart brightened. At home, he had begun reciting the names for Uncle Zhao as well as Aunt Yu, but they had sent him away before he could finish. After about twenty names, they would always say, dismissively, 'Okay, good. Now go play.'

Little Auspicious was really happy about Mr Tan's challenge. It would be a good opportunity for him to show off his skills.

'How about it? Do you dare?' asked Mr Tan.

Little Auspicious stood up from the bench. 'Are you serious about this?'

Mr Tan relit his extinguished pipe. 'Yes. One hundred will do, instead of one hundred and eight.'

Adults should neither overestimate nor underestimate the ability of children.

'Okay. Don't forget to count!' Little Auspicious began to recite the name of the heroes from *Water Margin*: 'Timely Rain Song Jiang, Jade Qilin Lu Junyi, Wisdom Star Wu Yong, Entering Cloud Dragon Gongsun Sheng, Big Sword Guan Sheng, Leopard Head Lin Chong, Thunderbolt Qin Ming, Double Whip Hu Yanzhuo, Small Li Guang Hua Rong...'

At first, no one thought much of it, and neither did Boss Tan. But by the time Little Auspicious got to Xie Zhen and Xie Bao, Boss Tan realised that the child before him was not playing around. His fluency and lack of hesitation amazed Boss Tan. His classmates also were surprised that Little Auspicious, who was usually inconspicuous, had such abilities. The three of them counted loudly, and their voices attracted many people to the shop.

Little Auspicious became more and more energetic. When he recited 'Mother Tiger, Mrs Gu', the boss raised his hand and said, 'Okay, you don't need to recite it anymore. It's all right; it's all right. Not bad!'

Little Auspicious knew that he had already recited a hundred and one names, and that he needed only seven more to finish the list. But he stopped to save Boss Tan some face.

Everyone applauded Little Auspicious. Boss Tan said, 'Okay. I'll give you fifty vouchers. Each voucher can be used to read a book for free.' Boss Tan had originally promised that if Little Auspicious or any of the others were able to recite the names, they would be allowed to read twenty books for free. But giving Little Auspicious fifty book vouchers demonstrated that Boss Tan was a very straightforward person.

Little Auspicious took the vouchers from Boss Tan. Each voucher had the name 'Little People's Bookstore' and was stamped with the word 'Free' in green ink.

Little Auspicious gave ten vouchers each to Song Xiaohui and his other two friends, and he kept twenty vouchers for himself. When giving them book vouchers, Little Auspicious suddenly realised that he had been too narrow-minded about Song Xiaohui reading his book.

CHAPTER THIRTY

Forgive me, Little Xinzi

Little Auspicious progressed to a new grade. The new class teacher was Ms Yuan. Her teaching style was serious and respectful but also very strict.

One day, Ms Yuan distributed marked Chinese literature test papers to everyone. The results of all the other subjects in the mid-term exam had come out, but the Chinese results were the last to be released. Ms Yuan stood in the gap between the podium and the desks, slowly scanning the students' faces with her scorching gaze, then she threw the papers on the desk of a classmate in the first row. There was a long silence, followed by a single word: 'Distribute!'

Everyone's heart suddenly sank. They understood that the results for this exam must have been unsatisfactory. Now, the grades were written all over Ms Yuan's face. The corners of her eyes quivered slightly, which was a sign that someone had failed.

Little Auspicious took the paper, closed his eyes, and said to himself, 'God bless, God bless.' Then he opened his eyes suddenly and took a long breath. The sound of exhalation came from all directions in the classroom as if everyone was doing breathing exercises.

Little Auspicious stretched his neck. Sitting in front of him on the left was Little Xinzi, whose formal name was Hao Yuxin. Her papers were upside down on the desk. Sitting in front of Little Auspicious on the right was Liu Guangting, whose papers were also upside down.

The teacher called Liu Guangting's name. He stood up.

'Liu Guangting, how many points did you get?' the teacher asked him knowingly.

'One hundred.'

'Okay! Very good! Sit down.' Ms Yuan's voice was rarely soothing and kind.

Suddenly, she became serious again, and she raised her voice. 'But some of our classmates failed in Chinese, which has prevented our class from becoming an advanced class collectively. Rat droppings that ruined a pot of soup!'

The students involuntarily looked left and right and began to talk in low voices. Little Xinzi lowered her head, her body trembling slightly.

Little Auspicious lived on the same alley as Liu Guangting and Little Xinzi. When they had first entered primary school, they had played together as freely as they had before they started school. In the fifth grade, however, they gradually drew apart because Little Xinzi was a girl.

Little Xinzi's life at home was very difficult. Her father had died of an illness, and her mother raised her along with her younger brother, who was too young to attend school. Besides making matchboxes, her mother also took care of a nursing baby. Little Xinzi was the only student in the class who was exempted from paying tuition and miscellaneous fees.

Little Xinzi's academic performance was very poor. She never spoke in class, and she always looked at the blackboard in a daze. When the teacher asked her a question, she would often be tongue-tied. Little Auspicious knew that Little Xin-zi cooked when she went home and that she also helped her mother make matchboxes.

During the class break, Shi Maomao, who was sitting in the back row, stood up and walked to the front. He claimed to be a descendant of Nine Dragon Tattooed Shi Jin, a hero in *Water Margin*. Usually, after class, he would knock classmates on the head with a small stick and poke their arms while shouting, 'Nine Dragon Tattooed Shi Jin is here. Take this staff!'

As he walked up to the podium, Shi Maomao picked up the chalk and wrote two crooked words on the blackboard: 'rat droppings'. Little Xinzi curled up her seat like a little mouse, with her head down. She knew he was referring to her.

Little Auspicious sympathised with Little Xinzi, but he didn't dare show it. Because whoever helped a female class-mate would lose his prestige in the class. Little Auspicious saw Liu Guangting's angry eyes. Liu Guangting's health was bad. His nickname was 'Little Fat Liu Guangting'. After running only a short distance, he would be out of breath from exhaustion.

Shi Maomao really pushed the boundaries. Today's incident gave him the idea for a new game that he found particularly amusing. Between classes he went around yelling, 'Rat poo! Rat poo! Have any of you ever seen rat poo like that?

Little Auspicious suddenly came up with what he thought was a brilliant idea. He called Liu Guangting out of the class-room and told him his idea. Liu Guangting opened his eyes wide and asked, 'Would it work?'

Little Auspicious nodded.

After the exercises between classes, a few boys huddled to-gether around the corner to play. Little Auspicious said, 'Hey! Let's read our names backwards. It will be fun!'

'Okay!' Everyone agreed. Shi Maomao didn't pick up on the trick, so he also shouted his agreement. Little Auspicious was first to read his name backwards. 'My name is Little Auspicious, but if you read it backwards, it becomes Auspicious Little.' Everyone became interested. Liu Guangting read out his name. 'Hee hee! Ting Guang Liu!' Everyone laughed for a while. Then it was Shi Maomao's turn. 'Maomao Shi'. Everyone burst into laughter because it meant 'little poo'. Shi Maomao took a long time to comprehend. He blushed but then pretended to be indifferent, saying, 'What's so funny about that?' But everyone saw through him and laughed even harder while shouting, 'Maomao Poo'.

From then on, Shi Maomao never called Little Xinzi 'rat poo'. He was afraid to mention poo in front of the others.

When they returned from school and arrived at the entrance of Xiaocheng Alley, Little Auspicious and Liu Guangting walked in front, and Hao Yuxin followed. As they approached Liu Guangting's house, Little Auspicious heard Little Xinzi calling his name. Seeing that there were no other students in the alley, Little Auspicious and Liu Guangting stopped and waited for her.

Little Xinzi walked up to Little Auspicious. Her eyes were red. She said, 'I know you two are good to me.' As she spoke, her tears fell to the ground. Little Auspicious and Liu Guangting panicked. It took them a while to realise that she was referring to the rat poo incident.

'How did you know?' Little Auspicious asked.

'I saw it myself.' Little Xinzi replied.

'Oh!' Little Auspicious breathed a sigh of relief. 'But don't tell anyone else!'

Just then, Little Auspicious saw Shi Maomao walking into the alley. He hardly ever went home through this alley.

Little Auspicious's face was burning, and suddenly he felt annoyed by Little Xinzi. Why did she have to stand next to them?

Shi Maomao coughed softly and slid past Little Auspicious like a fish. An unknown fire ignited in Little Auspicious's heart. He said to Little Xinzi, 'From now on, don't look for us!' Little Xinzi blushed and left them.

Something unexpected and embarrassing happened to Little Auspicious in his composition class.

Ms Yuan walked up to the podium and said slowly, 'Everyone, open your workbooks and put them on the table. I want to check the composition I assigned last week.' The students opened their books and put them on the table.

Ms Yuan stepped down from the podium and carefully inspected the work belonging to the first two rows of students. Then she stepped back onto the podium, set her eyes on the other four rows of students, and asked gently and with dignity, 'Did everyone finish?'

The classroom suddenly fell silent. The two rows of students who had been inspected all looked at Little Xinzi.

'Did everyone finish?' The teacher asked again.

No one answered.

'Hao Yuxin, have you written your essay?' The teacher's tone was doubtful.

'I finished mine.' Little Xinzi's voice was so quiet that they could hardly hear it.

'Okay! Read your essay then.'

Hao Yuxin stayed silent.

'Didn't you write it? Read it if you have written it!'

'It's not well written!' said Little Xinzi.

'It doesn't matter, as long as you have written it!' said Ms Yuan.

'It's okay. It's okay,' whispered Shi Maomao. He wanted Little Xinzi to make a fool of herself, so the class would have one more thing to joke about.

Little Xinzi read the title. 'My favourite person.'

'I like Little Auspicious and Liu Guangting the most...'

Little Auspicious could hardly believe his ears. She said she liked him and Liu Guangting! Little Auspicious felt the blood rushing to his forehead and his heart beating wildly. He felt that Little Xinzi was too annoying. Now, Liu Guangting and he were finished, and people would give them trouble!

After class, Little Auspicious's worries came true.

Shi Maomao shouted sharply, 'Wow! You guys are dating! "My favourite person"...'

Little Auspicious walked angrily up to Little Xinzi and said loudly in front of the whole class, 'Skinless and shameless, who made you like me...rat poo!'

Little Xinzi looked at Little Auspicious with surprise, her mouth half-opened as if she wanted to say something, but she couldn't say anything. Then her eyes filled with tears.

Little Auspicious felt a little regretful but still maintained an angry look.

Little Auspicious never expected that Liu Guangting would stand in front of him and say, 'Why are you swearing and bullying!' He shouted angrily and looked like he was about to cry, and his nose almost touched Little Auspicious's face.

The classroom suddenly fell silent. Little Xinzi was crying softly. She silently took out her workbook from her schoolbag, opened it, and tore out the page containing the essay she had just read. She slowly tore it and let the pieces fall to the ground. Little Auspicious's mind jolted. He really regretted his words. He bent down quickly to pick up the shredded pieces of paper, but a gust of wind blew them across the room. A classmate yelled, 'Hey! Give him a big boo!'

Shi Maomao was unusually quiet. He just kept muttering, 'Stop shouting! I was just kidding. I was kidding.'

A few days later, Little Xinzi's mother came to the school and told the teacher that Little Xinzi couldn't keep up with her homework and had dropped out of school.

When Little Auspicious heard the news about Little Xinzi, he felt a throbbing in his heart. He really wanted to see Little Xinzi.

After school the same day, he and Liu Guangting went to Little Xinzi's house. Little Xinzi was making origami. Seeing them coming, she looked very happy, as if she hadn't dropped out of school at all and as if Little Auspicious had never lost his temper with her. She brewed two cups of sugar water for her two classmates.

Little Auspicious couldn't help thinking, *Forgive me, Little Xinzi...*

CHAPTER THIRTY-ONE

Filming

One day in early winter, the teacher called Little Auspicious to the office, where two strange middle-aged people sat – a man and a woman.

Little Auspicious felt uneasy. The man said to him, 'Don't be nervous. Tell me what your hobbies are.'

'I don't have hobbies.'

The man asked another question. 'Have your parents ever beaten you?'

Little Auspicious shook his head and said, 'I'm not naughty. They don't beat me.'

The man smiled and let him leave.

Later, he heard that those two people worked for a film studio and had come to the school to recruit young actors. How great it would be to be an actor! Little Auspicious regretted that his answers at the interview were too superficial. He should have said that he liked to play the flute and the *huqin* (a string instrument similar to the *erhu*)! Although he was not very good, he liked to play them! Why didn't he say that?

A few days later, the school informed Little Auspicious that he was going to be in a movie. Little Auspicious was surprised and delighted. He asked the teacher, 'Am I still going to school?' The teacher smiled and replied, 'It's just one morning. Come back and continue the class.'

On the day of the filming, Little Auspicious, Song Xiaohui and several other classmates gathered at the school at half past six in the morning. Then they were transported by a minivan to the west gate of the Forbidden City, next to the moat behind Zhongshan Park. Everyone stood waiting outside the palace wall, not knowing what scene they would be shooting that day. The film studio workers adjusted the machine and made measurements with a tape measure. More than half an hour later, the director said to everyone, 'I will say 'Action!' and after that, you will walk beside the wall, just as if you are going to school.' Everyone nodded.

They did this three times. Then the director said, 'We are starting now.' Only then did Little Auspicious realise that the previous times had all been practice runs.

One of the film crew lit something that resembled a two-kick firecracker. When lit, the firecracker did not explode but, instead, began to emit white smoke from a small hole at the top. The air became foggy in front of them. When the mist thinned but had not completely dispersed, the director said, 'Action!' and they all walked on the road along the base of the palace wall as if nothing had happened.

The director said, 'The smoke we released represents the morning fog in Beijing. The children go to school, and the day in Beijing begins.'

They finished shooting the scene, thus ending that day's work. Although he didn't know what movie he was in, Little Auspicious felt that being part of the making of a movie was something to be proud of.

Sitting in Uncle Dong's yard that day, everyone listened to Little Auspicious talk about making a movie. Many children were there, including Lao Dezi.

When he described the two-kick firecracker that emitted smoke, everyone was very interested. They moved their bench closer to Little Auspicious's side as he spoke.

Then Lao Dezi said, 'Our school also went.' Everyone turned to look at him. Little Auspicious was very surprised. 'You also went to the Forbidden City?'

Lao Dezi shook his head. 'No. We went to the Summer Palace,' he said.

'Did you go too?' Uncle Dong's granddaughter Lao Pang asked.

'Our class went,' said Lao Dezi.

'What role did you play?' Uncle Dong patted him on the shoulder.

'We played the role of catching spies. The People's Liberation Army chased the spies, and our classmates helped the People's Liberation Army.'

Uncle Dong patted him on the shoulder again and said, 'Lao Dezi, are you telling stories again?'

'I'm telling the truth! I also saw people from Beijing Film Studio.'

The Beijing Film Studio that Lao Dezi mentioned was a compound in Baochan Temple Alley diagonally across from Dacheng Alley. It was the living quarters for the Beijing Film Studio, and many famous directors and actors lived in that courtyard. Little Auspicious had been there before, and the yard was very big, like a garden.

Little Auspicious knew that Lao Dezi was bragging again. He asked him, 'Who did you see? What did they have to do with your filmmaking? Who can prove you were there?'

Lao Dezi looked at Little Auspicious helplessly, with disappointment in his eyes.

Uncle Dong said, 'Okay, old Dezi, tomorrow I will go to Sigenbai Primary School and ask them if you have been telling us stories. What do you think?'

Lao Dezi stopped talking, and the children booed together. One of the children said, 'What do you think should be done?'

Lao Dezi's face turned red, and he suddenly burst into tears. 'Little Auspicious said he was in a movie. You believed that, but when I say I was in a movie, you don't believe it. Why are you so biased? Do you think I'm easy to bully?'

Everyone laughed. But Little Auspicious felt a little uneasy.

Little Auspicious seldom went to the cinema to watch movies. Not only did a ticket cost several cents but his parents also told him that the movies shown at the cinema were scary. There was a movie called *Midnight Singing*, which was said to have been exceptionally scary.

Most of the movies Little Auspicious saw he watched on the playground at Sigenbai Primary School. They showed a movie there every couple of weeks, and tickets were five cents apiece. Five cents was not exactly cheap. For that money, you could buy a sesame seed cake and a sugar ring.

Sometimes, Little Auspicious wanted to watch movies with Lao Dezi, but Lao Dezi would always say that he was not allowed to watch movies. One day, Little Auspicious's mother gave him a ten-cent coin and said, 'Buy two tickets. You and Lao Dezi can go to the movies together.'

Although the movie that day was very ordinary, Little Auspicious felt very pleased to see Lao Dezi happy.

Movies could only be played when it was dark, but after dinner, people would take small benches to the school to sit down and chat and watch the fun. They would watch the projectionist set up the machine and test it, and they would shape their hands into fox or dog heads so that the shadows would appear on the screen. There was a lot of shouting and laughing. The crowd gradually increased until it got dark.

When the movie was about to start, some children who had no money to buy a ticket climbed up the electric pole outside the school to sit on the wall. Others climbed onto the branch of a big tree outside the school. When they saw these children, the people setting up the movie would yell and drive them away.

The people who had bought tickets to watch the movie were on the side of the projectionist. In those days, even if they had no money, people still wanted to save face, so when someone yelled at them to go away, the children on the wall reluctantly got down. Only after the film had started did they slowly and stealthily reappear, but there were far fewer children than before.

Little Auspicious sat on his wooden bench, almost motionless. He was envious of the people who had folding stools. Those stools looked beautiful. Their canvas straps were soft and didn't stick to the buttocks even when people sat on the stools for a long time. Lao Dezi had also brought a bench. When Little Auspicious told him he liked the folding stools, Lao Dezi didn't speak but just looked at them with a smile. Then he said, 'The next time we come back, bring your family's camp bed, and the two of us can lie down and watch!'

Little Auspicious smiled. Lao Dezi had a rich imagination indeed.

Little Auspicious went to see many movies, including news documentaries, at Sigenbai Primary School. They would always play something else in addition to the movie, usually a news documentary. Whenever the audience saw a factory logo and labourer-farmer-soldiers appear on the screen accompanied by music, they would be very excited and would applaud enthusiastically.

The feature film that Little Auspicious watched the most was *The White-Haired Girl.* Every time he watched it, when it came to the scene where Huang Shiren went to Yang Bailao's house to press for debts, Little Auspicious couldn't help but look around at the audience, especially behind him. Why? He wanted to see if anyone would draw a gun.

When Little Auspicious watched *The White-Haired Girl* for the first time, he heard some adults talking about that scene. They said how, one time when the scene was played, a soldier in the audience was filled with righteous indignation. He couldn't stop himself from pulling out his pistol and aiming it at Huang Shiren!

Little Auspicious heard two versions of the story. One was that this occurred at stage production. Just before the soldier fired at the actor playing Huang Shiren, his instructor sitting next to him quickly lifted up the soldier's gun. The bullet flew over the head of the actor! The soldier was put in jail immediately after. Afterwards, however, the head supervisor said that the soldier had a high awareness of class struggle and a strong hatred for the enemies of the people. He was not only released but he was also rewarded.

The second version of the story had the soldier drawing his gun and shooting at Huang Shiren, leaving a hole in the screen.

Now, whenever *The White-Haired Girl* was shooting, shooting at Huang Shiren happened frequently.

After hearing these stories, Little Auspicious was very worried this might happen again and wanted to see if there was anyone in the audience who might shoot. He knew that the people watching the movies were ordinary people and that, therefore, they might not have guns, but they could still throw stones. But Little Auspicious's worries seemed unnecessary. During the times that *The White-Haired Girl* was shown at Sigenbai Primary School, the audience was very quiet and attentive, even though they had seen it several times.

The projector was very mysterious – almost magical. When the projectionist loaded the film, the film went from a reel on the left to another on the right. At the flick of a switch, the machine would start rattling. Little Auspicious thought that rattle was one of the most beautiful sounds in the world.

At these playground screenings, it was a common occurrence for the movie to stop unexpectedly. When this happened, people in the audience would express their dissatisfaction and wait anxiously for the movie to resume. Everyone wanted to know why it had stopped. Sometimes the film had broken, and it would take three to five minutes to be reconnected. Other times, after waiting for a long time, people would start to applaud sarcastically. When the problem was going to take too long to fix, there was usually no other feature movie to play because the next movie had yet to be received from the cinema, so the projectionist would put on a documentary to calm everyone down.

On one occasion, the film broke and not only did burning images appear on the screen but the projector also let out a low-pitched groan. There was some confusion in the audience, and many people stood up. Little Auspicious's first impression was that someone had shot at the screen. The people standing up may have the same imagination as Little Auspicious because the movie had stopped just as Huang Shiren threatened Yang Bailao to repay the debt with his daughter Xi'er if he didn't pay back the money.

But no one had shot at the screen. The projector bulb had become too hot and it had burned the film.

CHAPTER THIRTY-TWO

The Unquenchable Flame

One day, Lao Dezi came to Little Auspicious's house in a hurry, shouting, 'Auspicious, are you registering at Number Four?'

'Registering for what?'

'Filming.'

Little Auspicious followed Lao Dezi to No. 4 Dacheng Alley. It was the place where neighbourhood committees often held meetings. That day, extras were being recruited for a movie. It was a once-in-a-lifetime opportunity to be part of the excitement and earn money at the same time.

According to the regulations, only one person per family could go. Little Auspicious asked to sign up. A middle-aged woman said, 'Your family does not have a difficult life.' Little Auspicious said, 'It is quite difficult.' Lao Dezi reiterated, 'Their family has a really difficult life.'

The woman said, 'Then you can sign up. One yuan and fifty cents a day. There is work for a few days. Wait for the notice at home.' Only then did Little Auspicious understand that the payment was the same for everyone, regardless of their age.

'One yuan and fifty!' said Lao Dezi loudly and happily, patting Little Auspicious on the shoulder. There were nine children in Lao Dezi's family, and life was very difficult. This money would be a valuable contribution to his family.

Little Auspicious was very excited about this opportunity.

Little Auspicious went home and found a decent outfit. He waited, but the notice never came. But one afternoon, Lao Dezi ran to Little Auspicious's house and told him, 'After dinner, meet at the entrance of the alley at six o'clock.'

Little Auspicious and Lao Dezi went to the entrance of the alley ahead of time. Many other people had already gathered there. There were many people from the alley. Some of them seemed very embarrassed. Others, though, no matter how old or young they were, were very excited, as if they were going to be participating in a celebration.

After a while, a big truck came and took everyone away. After a long drive, the truck came to a stop in a very large open space. The passengers got down from the truck and looked around. The surrounding hills sloped down towards them. They appeared to be in a basin. Some of the adults said, 'This is the Bayi Film Studio.' Another adult said, 'This is the Bayi Film production *site* that makes the movies. This is not the film studio. If it is, why is there no house?'

After a while, two young men in military uniforms came and gave each of them a white cloth to tie around their head like a farmer's headscarf. They also gave each person a wooden stick more than half a metre long, with cotton rags wrapped around the tip. Everyone dipped their stick into a large kerosene barrel one by one and then walked up the hillside.

The person distributing the torches looked at Little Auspicious and Lao Dezi and frowned. 'Why are children here?' A man who came with them answered him: 'To play the role of the farmer's sons.'

Everyone laughed.

Little Auspicious and Lao Dezi followed the adults, wearing the white headscarves and holding the torches that were ready to be lit. Little Auspicious was very happy. If he was to appear like this in the movie, he wondered if he would look like a farmer. Lao Dezi said, 'You don't look the part at all. How can a farmer be as white as you? When they shoot a scene, they will ask you to stand back!'

They stood on the hillside and waited for a long time, but there was no movement. Everyone was getting impatient. 'Why are we here? Where are the cameras?'

It was getting dark. The flat area below them was illuminated by many lights. The main actors arrived wearing beautiful dance costumes. The women wore floral trousers and jackets, the men wore grey cloth military uniforms from the Yan'an period, and there were children with braids called 'sky pointing cones' in their hair. Gongs and drums sounded, and the place became very lively, but no one asked the extras to light their torches. Loud sounds of 'Dong! Dong! Qiang! Qiang!' reverberated for more than an hour, after which time the excitement had ebbed, and everyone began to feel tired.

Then a torch was lit on the opposite hillside, and someone beside Little Auspicious lit their torch as well. Little Auspicious lit his torch too. A cloud of black smoke rose from the flames.

After waiting all evening, the exciting moment had finally arrived! Everyone was holding up their torch to light it, until someone scolded them loudly, 'Who told you to light them?'

Everyone stopped. Only two torches were burning. And Little Auspicious's was one of those torches. He panicked.

The adult next to him who had lit his torch first panicked too and tried to put out the fire, but the torch had other ideas.

He rubbed the torch on the ground and stamped on it, but the flame was persistent.

Little Auspicious didn't have the same ability or strength, so his torch burned even more strongly.

The young man in charge of lighting the torches walked up to Little Auspicious and reprimanded him loudly. 'What's the matter with you?' Just then, Lao Dezi stepped up and said, 'I lit it for him.'

'You are mad! You shouldn't have done that! Get rid of it quickly.' Little Auspicious suddenly felt a surge of strength in his heart. He was not afraid. *When two people carry a stone, it is half as light*.

But the flame was tenacious and couldn't be extinguished. They tried all kinds of methods, but none worked The flames were still dancing, but with Lao Dezi's hand tightly holding his, Little Auspicious felt the strength of his partner.

They were still trying to find a way to put out the flame, but before they could succeed, the order came for everyone to light their torches.

It was about mid night when the truck returned them to the alley. Everyone gathered again at No. 4 to collect their money. By the time Little Auspicious returned home, it was already one o'clock in the morning.

This was Little Auspicious's first time earning money for his labour. His mother told him to keep the money for himself, saying, 'Don't spend it recklessly!'

A few days later, Little Auspicious asked Lao Dezi to go with him to watch a movie at the Xinjiekou Cinema. It was *The Wanderer*, an Indian movie.

The song in the film was really catchy, and they sang it when they got out of the cinema. 'Wandering everywhere—Wandering everywhere—'

When they came to the entrance of the alley, Lao Dezi suddenly asked, 'What if our families ask us where we went this afternoon?'

They discussed it for a long time and finally decided to tell their families that they had gone to the zoo and played in the afternoon. In reality, Little Auspicious didn't think that anyone in his family would bother to ask him where he had gone.

CHAPTER THIRTY-THREE

A Medal

One morning, Little Auspicious and Song Xiaohui were called to the office of the counsellor, Ms Zhao. When they arrived, there were ten other students from other classes already there. Everyone looked at each other a little apprehensively, not knowing what was going on.

Ms Zhao told everyone that in a few days' time, an international women's congress would be held in the auditorium of the Chinese People's Political Consultative Conference in Beijing, and that many distinguished foreign guests would be present. The school had accepted the invitation to undertake a major and glorious task – presenting flowers to foreign guests.

Little Auspicious and his classmates stared wide-eyed. Although they didn't know how important it was, they knew it was a great honour for them – only twelve students had been selected from the whole school!

Ms Zhao's eyes sparkled behind the glasses. 'You were selected from hundreds of Young Pioneers at this school! You are going to present flowers on behalf of the children in Beijing and the whole country! I envy you!'

Ms Zhao took out several stacks of clothes from a cabinet and unfolded them in front of everyone. The students' eyes lit up. What beautiful and high-quality dresses! The shirt was snow-white and made of silk; the trousers and skirts were woollen; the trousers were beige with some dark stripes; and the red scarf was made of satin. It was larger than Little Auspicious's scarf, the edges of which were frayed.

'The clothes you will be wearing are provided by your leaders. The Young Pioneers of the Soviet Union wear such clothes.'

On the day of the flower presentation, the students got changed in Ms Zhao's office. Little Auspicious wore beige suit trousers with dark stripes and a white silk shirt with lantern sleeves like those worn by princes in stage productions. Little Auspicious had never worn such expensive clothes before.

A bus took the students to the auditorium. The auditorium was on Zhaodengyu Road, not far from Little Auspicious's house.

Song Xiaohui was selected to present flowers to the president of the Women's International Democratic Federation, Madam Eugénie Cotton, who was from France. Others would then present their flowers one by one. When the band started to play, Little Auspicious and his classmates ran into the auditorium through the side door. He was the last in line. They had rehearsed this presentation several times the day before. However, unexpectedly, there was one less foreign guest on the rostrum that day. Little Auspicious looked around and saw that all the foreign guests on the podium had flowers and that there was no one for him to give flowers to. He had to give them to an old lady who already been given flowers.

By the time he ran off the stage, the other students had already left through the side door. Little Auspicious hurriedly followed them out. When he caught up with them, he found them all crowding around Song Xiaohui to look at something.

Madam Cotton had given Song Xiaohui a tiny, bronze-coloured iron model of a tower. It was the size of a little finger. (They later learned that it was called the Eiffel Tower.) The little tower had a fine chain attached to it so that it could be worn as an ornament. Everyone was so envious of her!

After a while, the side door opened, and those ladies with blonde hair and blue eyes came out of the auditorium. Led by Ms Zhao, Little Auspicious and his classmates applauded them enthusiastically. Some of the ladies took exquisite medals out of their pockets and handed them to the children. Others handed out small kraft paper packages which contained many medals.

A few minutes later, Little Auspicious had six souvenir medals in his hands.

Sitting on the bus back to school, the students counted the gifts they received and passed them around to each other. Among Little Auspicious's gifts was a particularly beautiful one – a silver-white commemorative medal of the territory of Poland. A small red bead was inlaid to denote Warsaw, the capital, and the medal was fired with enamel. There was a small beam connected by a small copper chain, so that the medal could be worn.

Back at school, when everyone was changing their clothes, Ms Zhao said in a serious voice, 'The souvenirs you got today, including the medals, must be handed over to the school and placed in the school's memorial room. Because you were not presenting flowers on your own behalf.' The room suddenly fell silent. No one spoke. Little Auspicious was very annoyed. Why did he have to hand it in? Could they not at least keep *one*?

Little Auspicious especially liked the Poland medal. He thought very carefully about what he would do. He decided he would hide it and hand in the other five medals. But as soon as he had this idea, Little Auspicious began to feel guilty.

Was doing this the same thing as stealing? What if the teacher found out? Where could he hide it?

Little Auspicious finished getting changed into his school clothes. He held the Poland medal lightly in his hand as he put the clothes and the other five medals on the table in front of Ms Zhao.

Little Auspicious didn't open his hand until he had left the school grounds. When he did, the medal was covered in sweat. Now that he had it, he no longer felt happy. Instead, he was in torment. Would the teacher find out? How big a mistake had he made? Little Auspicious spent the day in a state of anxiety.

By the next afternoon, he couldn't stand it anymore. He went to the office, pretending to be very casual, and said to Ms Zhao, 'I forgot to hand in one of my medals yesterday.'

Ms Zhao was chatting with some other teachers. It seemed as if it didn't matter to her whether Little Auspicious had handed it over or not. She pointed to the table and said, 'Leave it there.'

He placed the medal on the table and walked out of the office, feeling relaxed, relieved and even a little regretful. He didn't know if what he had done the day before was wrong, and now he didn't know if he had really done the right thing by handing over the medal.

CHAPTER THIRTY-FOUR

A Bottle of Soda

When it came to drinks, Little Auspicious was the same as every other child: he knew only Arctic Ocean soda and jasmine tea. But he could not drink soda as regularly as he wanted to, because soda cost ten cents a bottle. When the school organised outings for the students in spring and autumn, most children brought their own water.

The extracurricular activities of Beishi Erxiao were varied and engaging. One Saturday, five male students from Number Four Boys' Middle School in Beijing came to the class. The head teacher told everyone that these boys were now their temporary counsellors and that they would be taking everyone to visit their school the next day.

(Most schools in Beijing were divided into boys' and girls' schools, for example, Number One Middle School for boys, Number One Middle School for girls, Number Two Middle School for Boys, and Number Two Middle School for girls, and so on.)

There were seven students in Little Auspicious's group. The counsellor assigned to them was a freshman surnamed Feng. In the eyes of primary school students like Little Auspicious, the older students looked just like adults.

The counsellor shook hands with Little Auspicious and each of the classmates in his group. Everyone excitedly asked him, 'Counsellor, what are we playing tomorrow?' Counsellor Feng smiled and said to them, 'Tomorrow, I will teach you to make soda!'

At eight o'clock the next morning, Little Auspicious, Liu Guangting, Chen Yanping and the rest of their classmates gathered at the school gate. Counsellor Feng led them to Number Four Boys' Middle School near Ping'anli. They walked for about an hour. Little Auspicious had heard people say that Number Four Boys' Middle School was the best middle school in Beijing. When he saw it for the first time, his first impression was that it was very quiet.

Counsellor Feng led everyone into the chemistry laboratory. It was the first time Little Auspicious had ever seen a laboratory. There were bottles, jars, flasks, test tubes, and jars on the shelves. The students looked forward to making their own soft drinks.

At an experiment table, Counsellor Feng took out two fist-sized glass bottles, both of which contained 'medicine'. He told everyone that the white powder in one of the bottles was sodium bicarbonate – baking soda – the same powder that was used to make steamed buns and noodles.

The substance in the other bottle had a nice fruity sour smell. It was called citric acid.

There was white sugar and several empty soda bottles on the table next to a smaller bottle. Counsellor Feng pointed to the little bottle and said, 'That bottle contains essence. Just one drop can make the whole room smell good!'

The students watched him attentively as he began the demonstration.

He put several spoonfuls of white sugar into a pot of cold water for later use. Then he dissolved a little baking soda in

a bottle and added a drop of essence. He dissolved the citric acid in cold water and poured some in. Little Auspicious noticed that these ingredients took up only the bottom part of the bottle. Finally, the counsellor filled the bottle with the cold sugar water. When the bottle was almost full, he quickly tightened the cap.

The water in the bottle began to bubble, and then it seemed to boil.

Counsellor Feng told them that a chemical reaction was taking place in the bottle. He said that the baking soda and water had started fighting, and as a result, carbon dioxide was being produced. The citric acid would give the soda a very sweet taste. He also said that if they wanted to make an orange-flavoured soda, they could add some orange juice.

Everyone stared in fascination at the 'boiling' soda bottle. After a while, the water inside calmed down. Then the counsellor said, 'Right now, the pressure in the bottle is still very high. There is a lot of gas compressed inside. Sometimes when you open the cap, there will be a hissing sound and water will spray out. Some of the gas is still dissolved in the water, and when we drink it, it comes out of the water, making us hiccup: "uh uh—"'. Counsellor Feng imitated the sound of hiccups, and everyone laughed.

He opened the bottle of soda that he had just made so that everyone could taste it. Everyone quickly took a couple of sips, and there was no one who didn't yell while drinking. When Little Auspicious tried it, he first noticed a 'spicy' taste, and then a fruity, sour taste. *Awesome*, he thought. It was almost the same as the soda bought from a shop!

Next, under the guidance of Counsellor Feng, each student took a soda bottle and started to make their own soda. He weighed out on the scales the correct amount for each ingredient. When the time came to pour the water into the bottle to start the 'battle', each student was a little nervous and asked him to guide them.

Everyone was successful at creating a soda. Then they drank what they had made. The students all admired Counsellor Feng as a big brother.

Chen Yanping took the soda he had made and said to Counsellor Feng, 'If you open the lid, won't it taste bad?' Counsellor Feng looked at him strangely. 'Just open the lid and drink it. When the gas runs out, it will lose its taste. For soda, the gas is all you need!'

Chen Yanping turned around and picked up the water bottle he had brought with him. 'I want to pour the soda into my water bottle and take it home to drink.'

Everyone told him, 'It's so good that you should drink it now'; 'It would be a waste to wait!'; 'Don't wait until you get home.' After a few minutes, they quietened down. But Chen Yanping wouldn't be swayed; he wanted to take the soda home. Perhaps he wanted to give it to his mother. Everyone gradually understood that that was what he wanted to do, but they didn't say it.

Counsellor Feng was very considerate. He took Chen Yanping's aluminium water bottle and made another soda drink in it for him. He tightened the bottle cap and said, 'Don't shake it before you open it at home. Let it sit for a while.'

Some of the students were jealous. If they had known this was going to happen, they would have also brought a water bottle!

CHAPTER THIRTY-FIVE

Campfire Party

Children's Day activities in primary schools were always very lively. Every First of June, when Children's Day was celebrated, some students were always selected to participate in various activities in Beijing or the district. Generally, the students chosen were good-looking, had excellent academic performance or were the cadres of the Young Pioneers. When the class could choose only one classmate to participate in extracurricular activities, it would be Song Xiaohui. She was always selected.

Little Auspicious was sometimes selected, but such opportunities were relatively rare. That year's Children's Day, the class was asked to select six students to participate in off-campus activities. He was not selected. Although the activities organised in the school were very interesting, Little Auspicious was still a little unhappy.

During this First of June festival, the school announced that it would organise a campfire party. A big fire was going to be lit in the middle of the playground, and the students would sing and dance around it.

Originally, Song Xiaohui was going to perform a lotus dance at the party, and Liu Guangting an allegro. But because they would not be there, Ms Yuan asked the other students to sign up to perform.

Little Auspicious thought it was unfair. 'They went to participate in the "advanced" activities and have a good time there. The rest of us must perform here. Such bad luck.'

Then Teacher Yuan said, 'Little Auspicious, I heard that you performed the role of Mrs Zhu when you were in kindergarten. Let's put on that show here.'

Little Auspicious stood up and shook his head desperately. It had been okay to perform as Mrs Zhu in kindergarten, but now that he was in the upper grades of primary school, wouldn't it be too childish to play the role again? In kindergarten, he was bold enough to sing *Sister-in-Law Zhu Delivers Eggs* and *Little Son-in-Law*, but now he didn't dare to even think about it. Yang Guirong in the class could sing *Embroidered Gold Plaque*. Her voice was not only beautiful but also very high. Whether she sang in class or at a school party, she always received warm applause. How could his singing be compared to hers?

Ms Yuan saw Little Auspicious's pitiful appearance. He was on the verge of tears, so she stopped asking him.

Little Auspicious also became shy, especially around female classmates. He would blush frequently.

One grade below Little Auspicious was a girl named Wu Jingyi, who had performed gymnastics on the First of June the previous year. All the teachers and students in the school were full of praise for her. They found out later that her parents belonged to an acrobatic troupe. From that day on, when Little Auspicious saw Wu Jingyi at school, he couldn't help but take a few extra glances at her.

One day, Little Auspicious was on duty at the school gate. His job was to check that each student entering had brought with them the required handkerchief, water bowl and mask. As he was doing this, he saw Wu Jingyi approaching from a distance. He immediately felt nervous, and his heart beat wildly. A minute passed, and another, then Wu Jingyi walked up to him. Little Auspicious really wanted to say something to her.

Wu Jingyi held up the three 'take-ins' for him to see.

Seeing that her water bowl was a big enamel jar, Little Auspicious said, 'Your water bowl is so big!'

Wu Jingyi didn't say anything. She returned the items to her schoolbag and entered the school.

Little Auspicious had only to say a few words like this and it would make him nervous. If he were to go on stage and see so many students, especially female students, he would be very nervous. How would he be able to perform?

At the Children's Day celebration, Little Auspicious just wanted to be a member of the audience. On the way home from school, Chen Yanping caught up with Little Auspicious and asked him, 'Why didn't you sign up?'

Little Auspicious shook his head.

'Don't you know how to play the flute?'

Little Auspicious told the truth. 'I only know how to play *The North Wind Blows* from *The White-Haired Girl*. But I can't perform it in a show.'

'Let me ask you, what is that thin film you use when playing the flute?' asked Chen Yanping.

Little Auspicious felt invigorated 'The film is made from bamboo or reed. If you are particular about it, you can use garlic skin, which creates the best timbre.'

'And if you are not particular?'

'You can just use normal paper.'

Chen Yanping nodded. 'Oh, I understand.'

'Do you want to play the flute?' asked Little Auspicious.

Chen Yanping shook his head. 'I can't tell you yet.'

'You're so dull! If you don't want to say it, so be it!'

Chen Yanping thought for a while, then said, 'If you agree to perform with me, I will tell you.'

'You tell me first, and I'll make a decision later.'

'You promise first, and I'll tell you!'

'I don't want to play the flute,' said Little Auspicious.

'I'm not talking about playing the flute.'

'What are you talking about?'

'Blowing abacus beads.'

Little Auspicious was confused. 'How do you blow abacus beads?'

Little Auspicious followed Chen Yanping to his house and watched as he took out some abacus beads from a drawer. Chen Yanping took a small piece of tissue paper thinner than a page from a large-print book and pasted it over the holes of the abacus beads, and then blew into the holes. *Beep beep—beep—beep—beep—*

The melody of *North Wind Blows* sounded.

Little Auspicious told Chen Yanping that he would play the abacus beads with him.

They went to ask Ms Li the music teacher. She not only encouraged them but also told them that the first section should be a solo and the second section should be an accompaniment. Chen Yanping would play the main melody, and Little Auspicious would play the accompaniment by repeatedly blowing two notes. In the third section, the two of them would play an ensemble.

For the next few days, their cheeks were sore from practising.

At the campfire party on the night of the first of June, the first item was Yang Guirong's solo, *Embroidered Gold Plaque*, and the second was Wu Jingyi's gymnastics. The third performance was Chen Yanping and Little Auspicious blowing on the abacus beads. The microphone gave them an unexpected surprise. When it came out of the speakers, the sound of blowing the abacus beads was very similar to the sound of a tuba. The first song they played was *Morning Exercise Song*:

> The morning glow in the sky is like a hundred flowers blooming, and the birds on the tree are singing happily. How fresh the morning air is. How refreshing the morning wind is. We get up early every day and do morning exercises.

The bonfire was burning vigorously, and their faces were flushed from the heat. When the last two lines were played, all the students in the school joined in and sang loudly, 'We get up early every day and do morning exercises.'

When the two boys walked to their classmates to sit down, Little Auspicious saw Ms Yuan, Yang Guirong and Wu Jingyi applauding them warmly.

CHAPTER THIRTY-SIX

The Ice in Shichahai

One Sunday morning, the neck of the chimney in the Little South House broke, and when the wind blew, the smoke billowed into the house.

Their father asked Big Auspicious to go and buy a new one.

'Where can I buy it?' asked Big Auspicious.

'Go to Xinjiekou. Take Little Auspicious with you.'

Little Auspicious was very happy, but Big Auspicious was a little displeased, as if he had been wrongfully burdened, so he said reluctantly, 'I'm going to walk. Don't complain if you get tired.'

Their mother came over, put a cotton hat on Little Auspicious, and buttoned the top buttons of his cotton coat.

Little Auspicious went out with his brother. It was the coldest day of winter. There were small snowflakes in the air, and the puddles of water in the yard had frozen. You could ice-skate from the front door to the alley.

Suddenly, Big Auspicious said, 'Let's go to Shichahai first and then go to Xinjiekou from there.'

As soon as he mentioned Shichahai, Little Auspicious knew what his brother was thinking. Big Auspicious flew kites there in the spring, went swimming there in the summer and ice skating in the winter. But his brother hadn't brought ice skates with him.

'I'll take you to a fun place,' said Big Auspicious mysteriously.

Little Auspicious's eyes lit up, and his whole body was filled with strength.

They crossed Zhaodengyu Road, passed Baochan Temple and Huguo Temple, then passed Mei Lanfang's house. In the distance was Prince Gong's Mansion, where it was thought a high official was now living. The street began to curve to the right. They passed an embassy. At the end of the street, there was the back door of Beihai, which faced the Shichaihai.

Little Auspicious was tired.

Big Auspicious asked him, 'Are you tired?' but Little Auspicious didn't dare admit it, so he didn't speak. However, his pace slowed noticeably.

'We'll be there in a while,' said his elder brother, patting him on the shoulder. Little Auspicious followed him along Shichahai to the north. As they walked, his elder brother suddenly pointed ahead. 'Little Auspicious, look!'

He looked up. The world in front of him suddenly widened. He saw a large frozen lake. There were people and wooden carts on the ice. On such a cold day, you could still see the blue lake under the ice, because a section of ice had been cut out.

Several large square blocks of ice had been cut out, and people were pushing them far away.

Big Auspicious led his brother forward. Wispy white mist above the surface of the ice made it appear surreal.

A dozen workers with ropes on their backs were busy on the ice. They secured the blocks of ice with iron hooks attached to the ropes, then, gripping tightly with gloved hands, put the ropes over their shoulders and pulled the blocks over the ice. One worker bowed his body, tightening the rope, and pulled the ice step by step towards the shore along the paved slideway.

Little Auspicious was amazed. It was the first time he had ever seen something like this. He thought it was spectacular!

'What are they going to do with the ice?' asked Little Auspicious.

'By storing this ice in the winter, they can use it in the summer,' Big Auspicious replied.

'Where is it stored?'

'It is stored in the ice cellar. The iced soda and iced watermelon you drink in the summer all use ice that has been stored during the winter.'

A familiar figure appeared on the ice, pulling a piece of ice and walking towards the shore. Even though it was a very cold day, he was only wearing a jacket. The ears of his cotton cap were turned up, and a scarf hung down around his neck. When he raised his head, Little Auspicious recognised him as Dayuan, the grandson of Uncle Dong.

Brother, look, it's Dayuan.'

His brother was also very surprised. 'Ah, it *is* him. Why is he here?'

Uncle Dong's eldest son, whom Little Auspicious called 'Big Brother', was in his fifties. His eldest son, Dayuan, was a student at Nankai University. He was older than Big Auspicious. With a round face and a tall and burly figure, when you met him in the street, he looked like an adult. He was always smiling, and his eyes were calm. Little Auspicious and his brother were both surprised to see him that day.

Big Auspicious dragged Little Auspicious down from the shore. He ran to the back of the block and began pushing it. Dayuan turned his head and, seeing them, said, 'Hey! Who would have thought I would see you two here? What are you doing here?'

'Just watching the excitement. Why are you pulling ice here?'

'To earn money and gain knowledge!' said Dayuan. There were beads of sweat on his face. No wonder he was only wearing a jacket!

'You don't go to school anymore?' asked Big Auspicious.

'It's winter vacation.'

'This piece of ice is heavy, isn't it?'

'Three feet long, two feet wide, and two feet thick. It must weigh more than one hundred and fifty kilos!' Dayuan talked like a real worker.

Are the ice blocks all the same size?'

'They're all about the same size. It depends on how the ice freezes. If the weather is not cold, the ice won't freeze thick enough.'

Little Auspicious asked, 'Dayuan, where is this ice going?'

'The ice cellar nearby. There is also an ice cellar at Prince Gong's Mansion, but it is not used anymore.'

'Do you pull it all the way by yourself?' asked Big Auspicious.

Dayuan smiled and said, 'No, a truck pulls it.' When ice block was brought to the shore, a person came to meet it. Then Dayuan turned around and started to walk towards the ice. He took two steps and then came back and said to the brothers, 'Don't tell my family about my ice-pulling.'

The brothers nodded.

Watching Dayuan as he walked away, Little Auspicious thought that he was a chivalrous man. What was a chivalrous man? Little Auspicious believed that such a man must first have skills and, secondly, be modest. The students of Nankai University must be very capable, and yet this student had come to Shichahai to pull ice. No one would have imagined him doing this hard, exhausting work. Little Auspicious fantasised that Dayuan pulled ice as part of his training for martial arts, and he didn't want to tell anyone.

'You see, we didn't come in vain today.' Big Auspicious patted his brother's hand.

Little Auspicious nodded.

Just then, he remembered the small freezer in the home of his classmate Mei Jiali. One summer, he and Liu Guangting had gone to Mei Jiali's house to play. Mei Jiali's mother had given them a piece of watermelon each. It was icy cold and refreshing to eat. Little Auspicious asked, 'Was the watermelon soaked in cold water?'

Mei Jiali smiled and led them to a small wooden cabinet with beautiful patterns carved on its door. Mei Jiali opened the door of the cabinet, and Little Auspicious was stunned. The cabinet was divided into two layers. At the top was half a watermelon and several bottles of soda, and on the bottom was a foot-long block of ice cube with wisps of vapor rising from it.

'Where did this ice come from?'

Mei Jiali smiled, 'Every day, someone delivers it.'

Looking at the lake in front of him, Little Auspicious put these two things together. In the coming summer, the ice blocks in Mei Jiali's freezer might be ones that Dayuan has pulled.

'Brother, you can do this too?' Little Auspicious pointed in the direction of Dayuan.

'*You can do this too?*' said Big Auspicious with widened eyes. 'Remove the question mark! Of course, I can do this!'

Little Auspicious knew that his brother had great ambitions.

'Where are we going now?' asked Big Auspicious.

'Brother, we haven't bought the new chimney yet. Don't forget!'

CHAPTER THIRTY-SEVEN

Sister Went to a Provincial Area

When Little Auspicious was about to graduate from primary school, his brother and sister were about to start to work.

His sister didn't go to a factory in the suburbs. Instead, she got married. When she got married, Little Auspicious was still in primary school. Later, because his brother-in-law was transferred to another job, his sister went with him to Datong in Shanxi.

When he had learned that his sister was to leave home, Little Auspicious had suddenly felt empty in his heart. His sister had comforted him by saying, 'It's okay. Sister will come back to see you often.' Before she had finished speaking, she had begun wiping away tears.

For two years after his sister left, the end of each month was like a festival for Little Auspicious, because he would receive a small package from her. One package she sent him contained a book. It was Little Auspicious's first fairy-tale book.

There was a story in that book about a young hunter who rescued a dove from his net. Later on, the hunter was cursed, and he was about to die. Only if a church bell rang at midnight did he have a chance to be released from the curse. When all hope was lost, the church bell could be heard ringing faintly. It turned out that it was the dove struggling to ring the bell.

Little Auspicious's heart seemed to be gently nudged by that dove who had shown gratitude by returning the favour to the hunter.

Little Auspicious's sister had a small red wooden box with a copper lock on it. When she was packing her belongings into boxes, she kept Little Auspicious away from it. The more she did this, the more curious he became. He complained to their mother that his sister would not let him see the little red box.

When his elder sister and brother-in-law were about to leave home, she called Little Auspicious to her, opened the small box and said solemnly, 'Sister is leaving. Today I am giving you this box.'

Inside the box were some brand-new pencils, bookmarks made of leaves, a dozen cigarette cards, all depicting beautiful ladies in *cheongsams*, and two small notebooks. His sister took out from the box photos of the actresses Zhou Xuan and Xia Meng.

She said, 'I'm giving you the little box and everything in it.' When she said this, Little Auspicious couldn't help but cry.

His sister patted his head and said, 'You keep this little box for me, and you can return it to me when I come back to Beijing.'

Little Auspicious nodded and wondered: why should a mysterious box be opened? Once opened, there is no mystery. How wonderful it would be if he had never found out what was inside the red box!

CHAPTER THIRTY-EIGHT

Brother Became a Worker

When Little Auspicious was in the sixth grade at primary school, the state recruited workers, and his elder brother went to a factory in Baotou to work. Before he left, Big Auspicious gave him two bags of marbles from under his bed.

A month later, they received a letter from his brother. The address on the back of the envelope simply read *Mailbox No. XX*. The beginning of the letter read:

Little Auspicious's father put on his glasses and knitted his brows as he began reading.

Father and Mother, hope all is well....

As he read, he relayed to his wife that Big Auspicious said he was fine in Baotou. It was a secret factory, and he could not tell them details about his work. Little Auspicious's mother took the letter and said, 'This child is sensible, so you can rest assured that he will be okay, but his letter is too short!'

From then on, every two months, they would receive a letter from Big Auspicious. His letters became their comfort. A year later, his brother wrote in a letter that he was valued by the leadership and had been transferred to an important position, mainly doing welding work.

Everyone immediately thought of the master who repaired kettles and washbasins on the street.

Little Auspicious said, 'My brother doesn't weld tin pots!'

His father was happy. He touched Little Auspicious's face and said, 'Little Auspicious is right! Big Auspicious does not do electric welding like those people on the street!' That day at dinner, he repeated Little Auspicious's words three times.

In another letter, his brother told them that he had become the leader of the electric welding team.

His mother said to her husband, 'Big Auspicious is really promising. Did you discipline him too strictly before? That time you dismantled his pigeon cage, it was too harsh!'

Little Auspicious's father didn't speak for a long time. Finally, he said, 'How can you put it like that? It's the responsibility of a father to raise a child with great discipline. It's for his own good!'

In another letter, his brother told them that he had joined the amateur Peking opera troupe at the factory and was singing the role of the elder. Little Auspicious's father was very happy to read this.

There was one three-month period during which they received no letters. The whole family began to worry.

'Big Auspicious hasn't sent us a letter yet. Did you reply to his last letter?' asked Little Auspicious's mother.

'Of course I replied. The factory must be very strict,' replied his father.

When Big Auspicious finally wrote them a letter, he told his family that the leader had told him that his family had historical issues and that he was no longer considered suitable to work in a secret factory. If he wanted, they would arrange for him to work at an ordinary factory in Baotou – a tractor factory. At the end of the letter, his brother told them that he wanted to resign and return to Beijing.

Little Auspicious's mother looked at his father, who looked at the ceiling and seemed to be talking to himself, 'Oh! It's me who let the child down!'

He then stared blankly at the window, and it looked as if tears were about to flow.

When Big Auspicious returned to Beijing, Little Auspicious had already graduated from primary school. A year later, Big Auspicious found a job in a factory in the neighbourhood. He was not as naughty as before, but neither was he as fun. Little Auspicious didn't want to ask his brother about the transfer from the secret factory. He didn't know what to say to comfort his brother.

Later, when Little Auspicious had grown older, he brought up the past with his brother, asking him why he hadn't lost his temper with him when he broke the eagle kite. His brother simply said, 'It was also my fault. If I had glued some tissue paper to both sides of the wings, it would have flown. Hey! The kite was broken, and I could buy another one. But I have only one younger brother.'

At that moment, Little Auspicious's heart moved.

Epilogue

In Little Auspicious's house, there was a round coffee table with a glass fish tank on it. The fish tank was oval in plan, about a foot in diameter. It sat on a bright red cotton pad in the middle of a shelf carved from nanmu wood, and it made the room look lively. A craftsman had polished the sides of the fish tank into the texture of fish scales. Looking through the textured glass magnified and distorted the shapes of the goldfish.

Before his brother had left home, the fish tank had been in his room. In the winter of the year the Big Auspicious went to Baotou, he sent instructions in one of his letters:

> *Tell Little Auspicious that I still have two goldfish in my room and ask him to move them to his room for me.*

Little Auspicious was taken aback. He took the key and ran to his brother's empty room. He unlocked it and went in, only to find that the water in the fish tank had frozen. The two goldfish were entombed in the ice in elegant yet fragile positions.

Little Auspicious reached out his hand to touch the cold hard surface of the ice. The two goldfish had become beautiful ice sculptures. Little Auspicious was shocked. He should have remembered earlier. There was nothing he could do now. He decided to think about what to do with them when the weather became warmer.

Three years later, before Big Auspicious was to return home, Little Auspicious went to his brother's room. He had forgotten about the goldfish.

Their mother had lit a fire in the house.

Big Auspicious came back, and the first thing he saw when he entered his room was the goldfish. Little Auspicious's heart jumped into his throat.

The room gradually warmed up, and the ice gradually melted. He never dreamed that the goldfish would move. Not only did they move, they also actually started to swim! When one moved, the other also started to move...

First Draft: 30 August 2016
Second Draft: 13 November 2016
Third Draft: 27 November 2016

When I handed over the final draft of *The Auspicious Time* to the editor, I found that I still had a lot to write.

I didn't write about the oleander under the west wall. After the rain, dragonflies would fly in the yard, and some of them would fly on top of each other. We didn't know that this was love; we called it 'colourful fighting'. When dragonflies landed on the blooming phlox, we would walk up quietly and catch them one at a time. If you could catch a Plaster or a Laozier (two kinds of dragonflies with special patterns), that would be like winning the lottery.

I didn't write about the nail balsam. My sister would take off the petals of the nail balsam and smash them on a stone with a small wooden stick. In addition to painting her nails red with it, she also painted my cheeks. We laughed hard together!

I didn't write about the jade stick in front of Little South House. When I was one year old, a photo was taken of me holding a budding white flower in my hand. I had no pants on. The photo was placed under a glass plate, but the image was later affected by moisture.

I didn't write about the caterpillars on the jujube tree. The green caterpillar stung almost everyone in the family. When I recall the jujube tree, I remember the caterpillar as well as the crunchy and sweet jujube fruit. Looking at the caterpillar now, I think it looks very cool.

Thinking of these unforgettable little lives, the heart that seemed to be empty suddenly became full again.

Writing about my childhood has been my wish for many years. But when I finally picked up my pen to write, I realised that I had started too late. There were many things I could no longer remember, especially emotions, words, sounds and colours.

I have been away from that house and yard for fifty years. Many people and things have gone with the wind, and what is left has been fragmented. As time goes by, the stars gradually dim. In addition to time and distance, it is also because of the ten-year special period that destroyed the innocent trees and flowers there and damaged kind lives.

'Can't remember' and 'don't want to think about it' made me heavy and tangled my memory. I miss that place, but I don't want to go back; there are good times that I can't forget, and there are memories that I can't bear to look back on...

I looked at a magnolia plant at the corner of the building. It was already winter. There were no leaves, but there were buds on the branches. I really couldn't tell if it was the twilight of the magnolia tree or if it was ready to be reborn.

It is as if I am looking for spring flowers in the winter season. Although it is difficult, the blooming of life always surprises me!

I still want to write. Childhood is in the depths of memory when you try to awaken it. Sometimes it walks up to you like a stranger, making you wonder, 'Is this my childhood?' or 'Have I gone mad?' Sometimes it miraculously jumps up and hugs you, making you feel like a child again.

I am writing diligently. The 'dramatic' plots that life gave me that could be turned into stories have disappeared with time, especially those details and words. What is left is just one frame and one picture. What is missing is the moving emotional memory.

Some people say that the memories of great people belong to history, while the memories of ordinary people belong to literature. Although I am an ordinary person, the childhood stories in my heart also have a firm history. I don't want my readers to think that my childhood was spent in an era of nothingness. I hope they can see the past and a real childhood in that era.

I am writing with my heart. This is not a memoir, because my childhood still has the humanity and warmth that belong to literature, as well as the wisdom and culture that can enlighten life. Our hearts are connected. I believe that if my childhood is written from deep in my heart, it can also be yours.

Over the past few years, due to various opportunities, I have seen many writers write their own childhood books. I am interested in thinking about and discussing this issue, and I have learned a lot from the work of my colleagues and friends.

If you want to write childhood into a literary work, you must have appropriate fiction on the basis of reality. But many writers find that when they write, real life rejects fiction. But without fiction, there is no literature. I understand that the fiction here is actually the life I have felt and thought about. The literature I write now is the life I have experienced.

When I write about my childhood, I often encounter several problems: the relationship between major historical events and ordinary life; the relationship between heaviness and lightness; and the relationship between the child's perspective in childhood and the writer's frame of thought.

Through constant encounters and the overcoming of them, you will continue to gain a sense of success.

I also want to write about the culture of old Beijing, but what is Beijing culture? There are many kinds of Beijing culture: imperial culture, scholar-bureaucrat culture, civilian culture. The identity of our protagonist determines his cultural class, rather than following a Peking opera actor or an offspring of the Eight Banners to stand and cheer.

There is an old saying in Beijing: *The east is rich, and the west is noble, while the south is humble and the north is poor*. In the 1950s, although it was all Beijing, each region had its own culture and language. Some witticisms are very colourful, most of them are rhetorical questions, and most of them are used when people are being unfriendly. A conductor asks, 'Sir, have you bought a ticket?' The gentleman is not happy, so he replies, '*Have you bought a ticket?* Can you remove the question?' Another example: Person 'A' says, 'Hey, I didn't see—.' Person 'B' replies, 'You didn't see it? Are your eyes on your head for breathing?'

These conversations have their own characteristics, but they cannot represent the way that old Beijingnese speak. I think being old-fashioned and warm-hearted is a characteristic of old Beijingnese, and we have to be reasonable in everything. I do my best and don't try too deliberately.

I am still writing solemnly. I want to use this work to express my thoughts on my late father, mother and sister, and to my brother, who is still alive, and to my friends, and those good people who are sincere and kind.

Thanks to the editors Zuo Yan and Xing Baodan of Writers Publishing House. Thanks to those readers and friends who supported and encouraged me to write!

12 December 2016, Beijing

COMMENT

Gift of the Past

Li Donghua

Li Donghua, children's literature writer and critic. She has published more than 20 works, such as *Vera's Sky* and *Youth's Glory*. She has won the Bingxin Children's Book Award, the 10th Solemn Literature Award, the 8th National Excellent Children's Literature Award, the 13th 'Five One Project' Award of the Central Propaganda Department, the 2014 China Good Book Award, the Chen Bochui International Children's Literature Award, Shanghai Good Children's Book Award and other awards.

The little boy named Little Auspicious lived in Beijing from 1948 to 1957. For the Chinese, it was really a 'turned-up and generous' era. This great era falls into the eyes of a child, and after filtering through an immature heart, it is akin to picking up a drop of water from the sea or a snowflake from the whole winter. However, under the pen of an experienced and 'cunning' writer, a light snowflake is enough to lift the heavy winter. Mr Zhang Zhilu has a precise memory, as if Little Auspicious is still living in his body, and he uses Little Auspicious's senses to hear, see and appreciate from beginning to end. The things that this child cared about were very different from those of adults. Those grand events that adults paid attention to may have been unimportant in his eyes or even ignored. What he cared about was the trouble of not wearing a red scarf when he was nine years old; the eagles and pigeons in the stories of his elder brother; water buffaloes the size of fingernails. Fragmented stories link back to the small stones mentioned in the opening. When those scattered small stones are placed in a glass bottle and filled with water, they are reawakened by the water like a period of frozen time, glowing with colourful light, and this light is the refraction of the era.

For example, when writing about a mother-and-daughter beggar duo whom they often met on the way to kindergarten, the author did not fall into the cliché of 'all poor people must be dishonest and cowardly' but faithfully wrote about the strong characters of the mother and daughter who loved to scold others; perhaps this is the armour that poor people use to protect themselves. For Little Auspicious, he felt both sympathy for and fear of the two of them. After the founding of New China, Little Auspicious heard that 'both beggars went to a cooperative in the same street to make matchboxes'. One sentence lets readers see the ups and downs of personal destiny in the changing times, and then Little Auspicious's response was even more like 'I feel a burst of joy in my heart, and I don't have to worry about it when I go to kindergarten.' It is often such a childish stroke of genius that dilutes the heavy colour of suffering and hardship in life. For example, after Little Auspicious's family fell into poverty from being a wealthy family, his mother made a shirt for him out of parachute cloth. The shirt was airtight, and Little Auspicious was reluctant to wear it at first. Teachers and classmates mistakenly thought it was used by anti-Japanese pilots. Hearing this heroic story, Little Auspicious was full of pride and wanted to wear it every day, but when he learnt that the parachute had not come from an anti-Japanese hero, he was not willing to wear a shirt made out of a parachute. Being aware of good dress, he longed for a real white shirt, especially during choir performances. Finally, Mr Lao, the inventor in the yard, changed the parachute shirt into an umbrella so that Little Auspicious, who had always longed for a real umbrella but had no money to buy it, finally had a unique umbrella. In this short story full of twists and turns, there are projections of war, politics, and the ups and downs of fate. Underneath these uncertain waters, however, is the story of a little boy growing up, through hints, to quietly connect the ripples in the individual's heart with the turbulence of the times, with the sense that the unspoken words felt meaningful.

The Auspicious Time has the concise charm of a Chinese classical notebook novel. Although it is small in size, the characters depicted are numerous and vivid. Little Auspicious's family was a wealthy family who became poor. They lived in a very large house, portions of which they rented out when they were in trouble, so he got to know a lot of people. In addition to his own parents, brother and sister, there was a Japanese girl Sachiko who was a tenant, Mr Lao's family and others. The narrative extends from the small courtyard and then describes the neighbours around him, as well as the teachers and classmates he met in kindergarten and school. Mr Zhang Zhilu is good at writing characters; he is good at catching the decisive moments; and, often, he brings a person's character to life with just a few strokes. The protagonist, Little Auspicious, is a sensible, shy, but competitive little boy. He looked as delicate as a girl, so he paid special attention to his gender. When the kindergarten teacher asked him to play Aunt Zhu, he was very excited to be an actor, but he resisted dressing up as a woman, and this entangled mentality remained throughout his entire growth process. He didn't like to show off, but he recited one hundred and eight heroes from *Water Margin* in front of the bookstore owner with great pride. The female classmate Little Xinzi whom he never called by her nickname, as he was afraid that naughty boys would say that they were in a relationship; when Little Xinzi wrote in her composition that she liked him, he angrily berated her in public. He thought he was timid, but he didn't seem to miss the pranks, mischief, and mistakes a boy should make in his childhood. The author captures a boy's typical psychology, and *The Auspicious Time* is vividly written in a short space. In addition to Little Auspicious, the other supporting roles are all true to life.

'Auspicious' is probably the word most commonly used by Chinese people; no matter how the world changes or how a situation changes, the blessings that Chinese people give themselves and others will always be 'good luck and auspicious'. Using 'Auspicious' to name both the little boy who is the protagonist in the novel and the growing years that he experienced is not only a narrative strategy that kills two birds with one stone but also an unquestionable affirmation of the author's passing childhood. After a long time of washing, what remains in a person's heart must be the gold picked out of the sand, and that is also the best gift that the past can give to the present and the future. The author writes that Sachiko, a Japanese girl who lived in the yard, was always beaten by her father. Once, when her father wanted to beat her, Little Auspicious asked his mother for help, and his mother brought him to Sachiko's house. His mother did not mention the matter of being beaten; she simply asked Sachiko's father if she could measure the shape of Sachiko's shoes and praised her while measuring them, and, as a result of that distraction, Sachiko didn't get beaten. His mother's kindness and wisdom are highlighted in such small details. When you see the person next to you in distress, you immediately extend a helping hand, but you save face for the other person, and you don't talk about the other person's plight. In this novel, the reader can see the benevolence, warmth, understanding and sophistication of the old Beijingnese. Such details can be found everywhere in the book. For example, in the era of material scarcity, when visiting other people's homes, you must leave when it's time for dinner so as not to embarrass others. Little Auspicious's good friend Lao Dezi couldn't stand the temptation of Little Auspicious's dumplings, and he didn't leave at mealtime. Even so, he only ate one dumpling, and Little Auspicious glanced at him. This glance made the self-respecting Lao Dezi hurriedly leave. Later, when Little Auspicious went to Lao Dezi's house to play, Lao Dezi invited him to eat corn cakes regardless of the past. These little daily things have the beauty of human feelings hidden in them, and these simple expressions of humanity have clearly revealed a certain lack in people's hearts in today's world.

The writing style of *The Auspicious Time* is bland and peaceful, always filled with a poetic and warm atmosphere. It is an individual's childhood reminiscence writing, but it is not a personal nostalgic look back at the past. It tries to capture the lost beauty and the true interest of childhood in fast-moving times and to share it with today's children. We savour this piece together and treasure the precious moments.